Always and Forever

Dogwood Cove Book One

Julia Jarrett

Copyright © 2021 by Julia Jarrett

All rights reserved.

This novel is a work of fiction. The names, characters and incidents portrayed in it are the work of the author's imagination. Any resemblance to actual persons, living or dead, is coincidental.

Julia Jarrett asserts the moral right to be identified as the author of this work.

No portion of this book may be reproduced in any form without written permission from the publisher or author, except as permitted by U.S. and Canadian copyright law.

CONTENTS

1. Summer   1
2. Ethan   19
3. Summer   27
4. Ethan   39
5. Summer   49
6. Ethan   57
7. Summer   65
8. Ethan   73
9. Summer   83
10. Ethan   93
11. Summer   103
12. Ethan   113
13. Summer   123
14. Ethan   133
15. Summer   145
16. Ethan   157
17. Summer   167

18.	Ethan	175
19.	Summer	187
20.	Ethan	197
21.	Summer	207
22.	Ethan	219
23.	Summer	229
24.	Ethan	241
Epilogue		251
Acknowledgments		257
Also By Julia Jarrett		259
About The Author		261

Chapter 1

Summer

My dad is smiling at us, a smile of approval, love, and forgiveness. This makes him happy, seeing his daughter in love. My happiness is all he's ever wanted; it's the motivation behind his actions for all these years. It's why he let me go.

I turn to the man at my side. Looking up at him is like staring into the sun, feeling its warm rays heat me from the inside out. He's beautiful, strong, steady, familiar. He's home.

My eyes blink open as the dream fades away, courtesy of the obnoxious sound of my alarm. It's not the first time I've dreamt of my father in the years since I left home as a child, but this is the first time there has ever been another man in the dream with us. I have no idea who he is, but he is clearly important to me. I am caught off guard by the overwhelming emotions that stay with me even as I wake.

Tying my long blonde hair into a ponytail, I sit on the edge of my single bed in the tiny apartment I share with two other instructors from the yoga studio where I work.

I've always wanted to open my own studio, and I've got the training and experience to do it, but that would mean settling down. And no matter how hard I try to find a place that makes me *want* to settle down, I just can't. Even Calgary, where I've been the last few years, doesn't feel like home. It's just one more stop along the way, except I have no idea where I'm going.

When my phone rings, it's still early enough in the morning that I know it can only be one person. My mom lives several provinces away, in a totally different time zone, and she has never adjusted to the time difference. We don't talk often anymore, but every time we do, she seems to forget that midmorning for her is sunrise for me.

"Hi, Mom," I say cautiously.

"Hi honey, how are you? Where are you?" Her over-the-top cheerfulness grates on me. I can see right through it. She doesn't really care how I am, or where I am, she's just saying what she thinks she should say.

"I'm fine. Still in Calgary." My response is clipped, but she ignores it.

"Still? Wow, you've been there a while now," she titters.

"It's not so bad here." I rummage through my bag, pulling out what I need before I go to the studio to teach, my mind only half on the conversation.

"That's good, I guess. I could never stay somewhere that long. God, those years I had to stay in that damn town with your father were so hard. He never wanted us. I swear, leaving that pathetic town was the best thing I ever did."

Right on cue. Mom never wastes an opportunity to remind me how awful our life was in Dogwood Cove, the small town where I was born, and how horrible my father was. Granted, I haven't heard from him in the almost twenty years since we left, so I can only guess that the feeling is mutual. But my memories of my childhood aren't all bad. I've actually considered going back a few times over the years, not that I would ever tell Mom that, but something always stops me. Finding the time and money to go out west was only part of it; there's also the little girl inside of me who believes her father doesn't love her. Why would I go back to him when he has made it clear through his silence that he has no desire to have me in his life?

Still, whenever Mom tries to tell me that taking me away from my home was the best thing she ever did, I can't help but wonder to myself, *best for whom?*

"Did you need something, Mom?" I ask, eager to get the conversation over with.

"Can't I just call my daughter because I simply want to talk?"

"You could, but you never do," I say bluntly.

Mom just huffs and doesn't try to deny that it's the truth. "Fine. I guess I thought you might care to know that I met someone. Ralph and I are moving to Ontario next month."

This should surprise me, I guess, but it doesn't. Mom follows whatever guy she's dating anywhere he goes. Always has. And then when they inevitably dump her, or lie to her, or betray her somehow, she moves on. As a child, I was repeatedly dragged along with her.

"Okay," I respond, not sure what else she wants me to say.

"It wouldn't kill you to be a little excited for me, you know." Her tone is chiding, but I know she doesn't really care. "There's nothing wrong with finding a man and doing what it takes to make him happy."

Yeah, there is, Mom, when making him happy means changing who you are and blindly accepting his lies or false promises.

Mom has a pattern. And I'm sick of it. Have been for a while now, but she refuses to listen to me any time I try to convince her not to make the same mistakes again, so I've given up. That's why, for the last few years, I've been in Calgary and she's been in Quebec. I couldn't handle watching her make the same bad decisions over and over again. When I find a man and fall in love, it will be with someone honest and kind. Someone who treats me as a partner; someone who respects me.

Out of nowhere, the silhouette of the man from my dream flashes into my mind. *He felt like home.* That seems strange, to describe a person as home. But it's the only way to describe the comfort I felt in the dream. I can still sense his hand holding mine tightly, securely.

Too bad he is nothing more than a dream. A fantasy, even.

"Okay, sorry. I'm happy if you're happy, Mom." My words sound hollow to me, but my mother doesn't seem to notice.

"Thank you. Now, let's talk about when you might come for a visit. Niagara Falls is just lovely according to Ralph."

That's laughable. We haven't seen each other in over three years, and she thinks I'll just hop on a plane to Ontario? But that's my mother. Incapable of seeing anything beyond her own thoughts and whims.

"You know what, Mom, that sounds fun, but I have to go. I teach a class in half an hour; don't want to be late. Let's talk again soon, okay? Bye." I hang up with just a mild pang of regret. She might be a self-centered narcissist, but I still hate being rude to my mother.

After the unexpected call, I manage to get ready just in time to dash to the studio and teach my three classes for the day. Getting back to the house that evening, I find an envelope that's been slid under my door. The letter is from George Hendrix, Esq., and the header on the paper lists an address in Dogwood Cove.

The heavy feeling of dread in my stomach tells me this letter is going to change everything. I slide my fingers under the edge, ripping it open and pulling out a piece of heavy paper. I skim the words, and the envelope flutters out of my hand as I drop down onto my bed. My eyes blur over the page, and I have to reread it several times before the important part of the message sinks in fully.

I regret to inform you that your father, Carl Harris, has passed away. ...Your presence is required to settle a matter regarding his estate.

For a moment I consider just ignoring the letter. But something in my heart tells me that isn't the right answer. But what is? I can't bring myself to cry over the man who didn't try even once to reach out to me over the last twenty years. I don't feel sad, I feel numb.

And curious. Why would he name me in his will after all this time? Ultimately, it's curiosity that pushes me to accept that I can't just ignore this letter. I have to go back to Dogwood Cove.

A day and a half later, all of my belongings are loaded up and I'm sitting in my old truck, wondering who I need to tell that I'm leaving. Last night my roommates ordered takeout and helped me pack; they're all now at work. I've given notice to my landlord and the owner of the yoga studio and sent my mom a text that has yet to be answered, saying I was going away for a bit. And that's it. I honestly cannot think of anyone else to tell.

The reality is, I've got no one who will really care if I leave. In a way, that feels very freeing. I'm untethered, able to choose my path at will. It also feels incredibly lonely.

All the more reason to go.

My hand reaches back to touch the lotus tattoo on my shoulder. Out of something dark and dirty this beautiful flower rises. It's a permanent reminder that I can always change my life and find purpose and happiness. Of course, I have no idea exactly *how* I might want to change my life, I just know that I could, and one day I will.

Now, it's as if another piece of the puzzle is sliding into place. A piece that has a picture of a beach, a town square, and friends who used to be more like family.

Two days later, I wake up disoriented, and it takes a few minutes to remember where I am. Nothing is familiar, not the pale grey walls with nondescript artwork, the lamps that look like they're from the nineties, or the smell — a mix of mothballs and stale cigarette smoke. *Dogwood Cove...the motel off the highway.* Everything comes rushing back to me, from receiving the letter telling me Dad was dead, to the long drive to get here. Mental and physical exhaustion had me collapsing on the bed fully clothed last night, not even caring about the sharp springs poking into my back. With a groan I flop over onto my stomach, not ready to face the day. But eventually, my grumbling belly forces me out of bed. Bleary-eyed and desperate for coffee and food, I stumble into the tiny shower. After too many minutes letting the hot water stream down on my face, I quickly cleanup and get dressed. I have a meeting with George, the lawyer who sent the letter, at ten o'clock and I don't want to be late. But first, breakfast.

Leaving my motel room, I decide to walk the couple of kilometers or so that lead to the small downtown of Dogwood Cove. The late spring air is warmer than it was in Calgary, but it's still chilly enough that I need to zip up my jacket.

When I hit the main part of town, nostalgia fills me. This town is adorable, with tree-lined sidewalks, cute houses with tidy yards, and friendly people smiling and giving me a wave. No one seems to recognize me, but that's not surprising since it's been so long.

Wandering down Main Street, I spot a sign on the sidewalk advertising fresh muffins, and walk up to an adorable café with a blue and white awning. There's a sign painted on the window in swirly script that reads *The Nutty Muffin*. The name makes me smile, and the aroma coming through the open door is mouthwatering, a perfect combination of good coffee and fresh baked bread. My stomach rumbles again, louder this time, as I walk inside and join the short line waiting to order. I take a minute and look around, appreciating the comfy and cozy feel. Large, overstuffed chairs are centered around small tables, artwork lines the walls, and the chatter of happy customers gives the place a fabulous vibe. I can see myself spending a lot of time here.

I step up to the counter, still perusing the glass display case that holds several different flavors of muffins as well as donuts, strudels, and savory pastries, when I hear my name said in disbelief.

"Summer Harris? Is that you?"

I look up and into the eyes of Mila Monroe, my childhood best friend. She's wearing a T-shirt that says *The Nutty Muffin* on it, and her long brown hair is pulled back in a braid. She feels so familiar, I feel a small chip of my lonely heart repair simply from seeing her. She was more than just a friend, she was family.

"Oh my God, it is you!" she cries out, before rushing around from behind the counter and pulling me into a hug. My arms come up to wrap around her, as I absorb yet another shock, this time a pleasant one.

"Mila, I can't believe you're here," I say in disbelief.

"Of course I am, I never left."

Her words sting, even when delivered gently.

"I wish I had come back sooner." My voice breaks on the words. "My mom kept moving us and then I didn't hear from anyone, so..." I trail off. After all, how do you admit that as a kid, and then a teenager, you felt abandoned by not only your parent but your best friends, too?

Mila's face is wreathed in sorrow. "Ethan and I begged our parents to figure out where you were. I missed you so much. But your dad wouldn't talk about anything having to do with you and your mom for years. We had no idea where you were, if you still had his last name, any way to find you, really." Someone from behind the counter calls her name and Mila looks over, giving them a nod. "Listen, I need to get back to work. Why don't you take a seat and I'll come over when I can?"

I gesture over to the door. "I can't stay, actually; I have a meeting with a lawyer in town."

"Oh, right. You must be back because of your dad." Mila fidgets with her apron strings. "I'm really sorry about that, the whole town misses him."

All I can do is nod robotically. It's weird to hear that the man my mother always said was cold and uncaring was missed by people. It's uncomfortable, actually, as it makes me wonder if all this time she's been lying to me. Or at best, telling me her truth instead of the actual truth. But I can't go down that road yet. That would mean I missed out on years with my father. Years I can never get back.

Mila gives me a sympathetic look, and her hand touches my shoulder briefly before she bustles back around the counter and pulls two huge muffins out of the case, placing them in a bag for me. She then takes a piece of paper and scribbles something down on it.

"Let me at least give you some coffee and a muffin, and one for George. That must be who you're meeting about your father's will." She pours a coffee and hands both it and the muffins to me with a wink. "My nutty apple streusel muffins are famous around here; you're lucky you got one before I sold out. And here's my number. Text me yours, and then we can make plans to catch up soon."

"Thanks," I say, thumbing out a message to her with my number. I reach for my wallet to pay and she brushes me off with a wave of her hand.

"No way, girl. It's on the house."

Before I can respond, she's pulled away by another customer. With one last look at the woman I used to have sleepovers with, swap secrets, share snacks, and play with all day, every day, I head to the door. Back out on the sidewalk, I take a grateful sip of the rich, warm brew. Exhaling deeply, I let those first tendrils of caffeine-induced alertness fill me with the energy I'm pretty sure I'll need to get through the next thing I have to face today.

Time to figure out exactly what my estranged father wanted from me.

With a bushy white beard and kind eyes hidden behind glasses, George Hendrix looks more like Santa Claus than a lawyer. He's even wearing suspenders, for Chrissake. He sits across from me in a leather chair matching the one I'm seated in, his hands folded in his lap and a kind expression on his face.

"Mighty kind of Mila to share one of her muffins with us. She's a good girl, that one."

I nod in agreement, my mouth full of the delicious muffin. Damn, Mila can bake, and I can't wait to try more of what she's got at the bakery. After swapping a few pleasantries over our muffins, George finally pulls a file folder across his desk and opens it.

"Now, I'm not certain how much you know about your father's last few years, so why don't I start at the beginning," he says formally.

I swallow a chunk of muffin that has suddenly lodged in my throat. "Yes, please," I croak. "I don't know anything," I finish lamely.

To his credit, George just nods. There's no judgment about the fact that I know nothing about my dad's life.

"Two years ago, Carl was diagnosed with pancreatic cancer. Unfortunately, they didn't find it in time to be able to do any lifesaving treatment. But he was determined to fight any way he could. Oh, that man fought hard." George takes off his glasses with a chuckle, but I can see he's fighting his own emotions as he wipes at his eyes. "He also wanted to make sure that everything was in place for you, Summer. He and I met just two days after his diagnosis, and he had me write up the will and start the process of trying to locate you. I'm just so sorry we weren't able to do that in time. All he wanted was to see you again." Shuffling some papers, George finds the one he's looking for, and slides it toward me. It looks like a deed of some kind. "Do you remember Oceanside Resort? The old cabins on the beach?"

I nod slowly, skimming the paper and not really understanding it.

"Your father bought the property the year before he got sick. He had plans of renovating it and then getting in touch with you. He hoped you might want to come home someday and visit. He wanted a legacy for you." George pats the top of my hand. "He missed you so much."

I'm pretty sure my jaw hits the floor at this point.

"My dad wanted me to come home." I'll get to the whole *Dad bought Oceanside Resort* in a minute. Right now, I'm still trying to process everything he's told me. After all, you don't go from spending almost twenty years thinking that your dad wanted nothing to do with you, to hearing how much he missed you, without a bit of a mental adjustment.

George's eyes soften. "Oh yes, Summer. He very much wanted to see you. He missed you greatly, and the years your mother moved you around so much that we couldn't keep track of your whereabouts were torture for him." Sorrow is clear in George's voice, and something cracks open inside of me. This man, this stranger, knew my dad. More than that, he knew that my dad loved me and wanted to find me. The grief of finally accepting the fact that my father loved me, but I'm too late, hits like a tidal wave. George remains quiet, patiently handing me tissues as I cry, finally letting the grief of losing my father flow out of me. I've missed so much. Why didn't I find a way to come home sooner? All of my excuses feel weak, and I can't believe I let myself accept my mother's narrative when she told me Dad wanted nothing to do with me.

Eventually, I get enough control over myself to ask. "Are you saying Dad left Oceanside Resort to me?"

George nods and gestures to the paper. "Yes, Summer. That's the deed, which we'll get changed to your name."

Wow. I've gone from thinking my dad never loved me, to finding out he loved me, missed me, and left me a freaking beachfront resort to run, all in the span of five minutes. To say my head is spinning would be the understatement of the century.

"So, what now?" I ask tentatively.

George shuffles some papers on his lap before adjusting his glasses. "Well, I suggest you go and take a look at the property before you make any decisions. You should know, your father didn't have any money to leave you, only Oceanside. He spent all of his retirement savings purchasing the property, but then the cancer spread so quickly he never had time to see anything to completion."

I nod slowly, trying to understand what he's saying.

"When you get to the resort, try to have an open mind. The town would love to see it reopen, but it might be more than you can handle, and there's no shame in that."

Crap. What the hell did you get me into, Dad?

When I leave the lawyer's office and step outside, it's warm out. The sun is breaking through the clouds, and the rays of light fill me with my own light. I have to admit, the idea of running Oceanside Resort is stirring something in me — a sense of purpose and a drive to let myself imagine a future here in Dogwood Cove. Maybe the property isn't as run-down as it seems from the road, and I can get it open this summer. My mind drifts back to my childhood as I drive, and I remember spending time at Oceanside with Mila and her older brother. I remember buying slushies at the main building, and on a sunny day, the former owner would be grilling hot dogs on the back deck and selling them for a dollar. Mila and I used to spend a lot of summers playing on the sandy beach. There was a gigantic log that had rolled up on shore that was fun to climb over, and an old swing set that we were allowed to use, despite being locals and not guests.

But any hope of resurrecting those childhood memories is dashed when I reach the driveway to the resort. The sign is hanging by only one chain, and the paint is faded and peeling. Not a good start. I drive slowly down the path, dread building inside. As the buildings come into sight, I curse under my breath. They're a mess, I can already tell. Any hope of having the place open by summer is completely dashed by what I see.

Parking in front of the main building, I turn off my truck and take a good look around. All of my fond memories are now overshadowed by the unpleasant reality I'm currently facing. My eyes take in boarded up windows, a broken step leading up to the door, and badly peeling paint. There are weeds and trash everywhere, including signs of more than one bonfire right there on the ground in front of the building. Walking down toward the cabins I see more trash, more weeds, and more signs that people have been camping down here with little to no regard for the property.

The first cabin seems to be in slightly better shape, with actual windows and a door that doesn't appear to be broken.

"Oh my God!" I shriek when I push the door open and am greeted by multiple glowing eyes in the dim room. I close the door quickly and back away without getting a good enough look at what kind of animal has made its home there.

Before I can move on to any of the other cabins, I hear a horn honk. When I turn toward the sound, I see a large, newer model pickup truck pulling in and parking next to my beat-up old Chevy. Someone climbs out and starts to walk toward me. Despite being silhouetted against the sun, hiding his face, my heart somehow recognizes him as the man from my dream even as my brain questions how that could be true. But this scene — the sun that has broken through the clouds, the waves crashing behind me, and this man — it's my dream. My heart starts to pound, but I don't feel scared.

When he comes nearer, my breath catches when I realize it's Ethan Monroe, Mila's older brother and the closest thing to a brother I've ever had. But the man headed my way is not someone who inspires brotherly feelings. Oh no, the stirrings of attraction I feel as I take in his strong jawline, deep blue eyes, and tousled hair hidden under a baseball cap are anything but familial. His body fills out a pair of jeans and flannel shirt perfectly, giving him a scruffy, sexy, lumberjack vibe that is unexpectedly attractive. This is not the boy I ran around with as a child.

"Ethan?"

He grins, and walks right up to me, wraps his arms around me, and lifts me off the ground. Not hard to do, considering he's at least a foot taller than me.

"When Mila called me and said you'd just walked out of the bakery, I had to get my ass down here and see you for myself." He smiles down at me gently. "How ya doin', shorty?"

Tears threaten to fill my eyes at hearing my old nickname come out of his mouth. Stupid emotions. I give Ethan a watery smile, and he pulls me back in for another hug. This time I take notice of his warmth, and the solid planes of muscles pressed up against me. His hand rubs circles on my back that he probably means to be comforting. All it makes me want to do is arch into his touch. But that feels so strange, seeing as it's Ethan, so I pull back. These unfamiliar feelings must be a result of exhaustion and emotional overload. That has to be why he makes me think of the man from my dream.

Ethan's eyes widen as he looks around and takes in the disaster that is Oceanside Resort. "You've got your work cut out for you. I haven't been here in awhile; I had no idea it was still this bad."

He comes over to stand by me, and together we look down the row of beachfront cabins.

"It's a mess, Ethan," I say, my low voice betraying my emotion. He takes me by the elbow and propels me toward the first cabin.

"Okay, we can fix this. We'll get a work crew together and —"

Before I can warn him about that cabin's residents, Ethan pushes open the door. This time, the critters inside are angry enough from being disturbed twice that they flee, scurrying out the door with an angry hiss.

"Holy fuck!"

Ethan leaps back, stumbling down the stairs and banging his elbow on the way down as two raccoons run past him.

I start to laugh. I can't help it, the sheer insanity of Ethan, big, strong, manly Ethan, being frightened by a pair of raccoons has me wheezing, I'm laughing so hard. He stands there breathing heavily for a minute, then he, too, starts to chuckle. Eventually we're both laughing out loud. Only now, mine is a mixture of amusement and pure hysterics over what a massive pile of shit my father left me.

Eventually I calm down and drag in a ragged breath. "Ethan, what the hell am I going to do?" I whisper.

He walks over, gingerly rubbing his elbow. "I don't know, Summer. But we'll figure it out."

Hearing Ethan say the word *we* does something to me. For the first time in a long time, I don't feel alone.

Chapter 2

Ethan

When my sister said Summer Harris was back in town, I was excited to see the girl who was so close to Mila, and spent so much time with us that she felt like a second little sister to me. I felt like a part of our family had come back home. Nothing could have prepared me for the beautiful woman I found instead.

And now that woman is dealing with the loss of her father and the inheritance of a total dump. And I want to help. I can still remember one of the last times I was there to help Summer, back when we were kids. It was the year she moved away, so she was ten and I was twelve. Mila and Summer were up in the treehouse in our backyard while I mowed the lawn. For some reason, Summer wanted to climb down, but when she got part way down the ladder she fell. She was always a tough kid, so when she started to cry, I came running. Her arm was bent funny, so I held it in place while Mila ran for help. I remember her little body leaning against mine, and her tears making my T-shirt wet. I guess I've always wanted to protect Summer, to take care of her. There was never anything more than friendship between us back then, but I remember the pride I felt because she turned to me for comfort.

Being the one to comfort her now is different. Much more than friendship. This version of Summer, with strong curves, small delicate hands, and a quiet inner strength is confusing my memories of her as a kid.

I shake my head to try and get those ideas out of my brain. This isn't the time, or the place, or the woman for that line of thinking. Instead, I clap my hands together and put my game face on. "Alright, what do you say we finish taking a look around? You happen to be standing next to Dogwood Cove's all-around handyman. At your service." I finish with a bow, earning me a laugh.

"So, are we just going to ignore the fact that you were terrified by a couple raccoons?" she says.

I narrow my eyes at her, taking in the mischief dancing in hers. "Yes. Yes, we are. That's never to be spoken of again."

"Fine, you can pretend to be Mr. Giant Lumberjack, not afraid of anything, watch me chop down this tree..." She mimes wood chopping with her hands as I fight back a chuckle. "But I know the truth now. Woodland creatures freak you out." She nudges me in the side, and I want her to stay there but she doesn't. "Don't worry, I won't tell anyone."

She's teasing, but there's something more. If I wasn't so stuck on the fact that Summer is my little sister's best friend, and therefore totally off-limits for me, I would swear she's flirting.

"Tease all you want, Summer Harris, but you need me and my lumberjack skills if you want to get this place cleaned up." I fold my arms across my chest, adding an extra flex to my biceps. When her eyes flit over to my arms, I almost give myself a mental high five, then catch myself. *Fuck. Sister's best friend, man. Stop it.*

"Okay, I accept your offer. Lead on, show me what kind of mess I'm in." She gestures toward the rest of the cabins, and we set off.

Several hours later, we're both covered in dust, and there's a grim determination covering Summer's face. I grab a couple bottles of water from the cooler in my truck and take them back to where she's sitting on a rock overlooking the water. From here, it's easy to see the appeal of the place. The waves are breaking gently at the shore, seagulls are crying in the distance. It's beautiful. But behind us is a fucking shit show of massive proportions.

"The good news is, everything seems structurally sound. The biggest job will be cleaning up the inside of the cabins and the main building." I start, handing her the water. "Obviously some windows need to be replaced, a fresh coat of paint, a few repairs to railings and steps, but the actual renovation work doesn't seem to be too extensive."

"No, but the cleanup alone could take weeks. And money," comes her reply. The dejected tone in her voice hits me hard. She's a friend in trouble, and I want to help.

I wrap my arm around her shoulder again. She leans into me willingly, her head going to rest against my side. She smells good, peppermint and something else, something girly. And she feels even better, like she belongs by my side. But that's a strange feeling to have, and she must feel the same way because she suddenly sits up and shifts away from me slightly. "Shit, I'm sorry Ethan. You don't need me whining and moaning to you again." Her hand lifts up and scrubs over her face, covering her eyes. I reach over and pull it down, making her look at me.

"Summer don't apologize. I'm here because I want to be."

She doesn't respond, but her eyes are searching my face. Whatever she sees there, she seems to accept, because she nods, then turns back to look at the water. We stay like that for awhile, in a comfortable silence, and for only a second I let my mind drift to an imaginary place where Summer isn't Mila's childhood best friend, she's just a beautiful woman who I'm attracted to and free to pursue.

But my phone vibrates, interrupting that dream. A message from none other than my little sister, reminding me about dinner this Saturday. It's my turn to cook and she wants me to invite Summer.

"Hey if you don't have plans this weekend, Mila and I do this thing where every Saturday we have dinner together. This week is my turn to cook; I'm making fish tacos. Do you want to come?"

Summer mimes looking at something in her phone. "I'll have to check my very busy calendar." We both chuckle, and she nudges me with her shoulder. "I'd love to come, thank you."

"Great." I stand up and stretch my arms up. "Ready to check out the rest of these cabins?" I sweep my arm out ahead of me, and Summer gives me a small smile.

The rest of the afternoon I keep things light and friendly between us as we assess the damage, and I make a mental list of everything that has to be done. That list is daunting, even for me.

After leaving Oceanside Resort, my guess is that Summer is heading straight back to town. I, on the other hand, am in no rush to get back to town. Instead, I drive along the back country roads for a bit, eventually ending up at the end of a road overlooking some fields. When I cut my engine, the silence surrounds me and there's nothing distracting me from admitting to myself the glaring truth that I'm attracted to Summer Harris. All the years she was gone turned her into an absolutely stunning woman. Her skin glowed with warmth, even in the grey, dismal light of a rainy West Coast day. Those eyes that were too big for her face as a child now fit perfectly. They still shine like the sea glass she always loved to collect. Her hair is longer, and my fingers itched to take the blonde strands out of the braid she had it in and run them through it.

If she were anyone else, I would be asking her out on a date. But this is Summer. She's not someone I can have for one night and then move on. She used to be Mila's best friend, she used to be my friend. I have to remember that. Besides, the last thing she needs right now is any complications. She needs friends.

It's close to dinner time before I make it back to my office to finish up reviewing some paperwork that I abandoned when I went to help Summer.

Town hall is empty when I unlock the front door. The lights are all off, but I walk down the short hallway to my office on autopilot, the dim glow from the streetlamps coming in from the windows enough to guide my way. I've got the big corner office, a perk of being the Mayor of Dogwood Cove. I didn't ask for this job. My buddy, Reid, is responsible for getting me on the ballot, but I still try to do my best for the town. This is where I grew up, and I can't imagine myself ever leaving. Someday, I want my kids to run and play in the park, put on spring concerts in the gazebo, sneak ice cream samples from Sweet Scoops. All the things I remember doing as a child. Funny how so many of those memories include Summer.

I turn on the small desk lamp, letting the warm light illuminate my desk. Turning on my computer, I grab a protein bar out of the drawer. I've pulled enough late nights here that I know to always have snacks on hand. Being the mayor of a small town isn't such a huge job, but when I consistently put it last behind helping my sister, dealing with the properties we own around town, and generally finding anything to do to keep me out of this damn office, well...late nights happen.

Once the home screen on my computer is finally loaded, I sit down to catch up on everything. There's the usual list of permit applications, council issues, and a smattering of complaints about road repairs and services the town needs. Most I can deal with quickly, with either a stamp of approval or a signature. The simple tasks can be done on autopilot, which means most of my mind is free to think about Summer. Her coming back after all this time feels important somehow. In more than just a reuniting with an old friend kind of way. She's facing a lot right now, and I want to make it easier for her any way that I can, so I grab my phone and dial my sister.

"Hey Mills, is the apartment over the bakery still vacant?" I ask without preamble.

"Nice to talk to you, too, big brother. I'm fine, thank you," comes her snappy reply.

"Sorry. Mila, dearest sister of mine, I do hope you had a lovely day. Could you perhaps tell me if the apartment over your bakery is vacant?" I inject an over-the-top fake nice tone to my voice.

Mila just huffs out a sigh. "Don't be a jerk. Yeah, it's empty. Why?"

"Because we should offer it to Summer," I say casually.

"Huh."

"What does that mean?"

"Nothing, I'm simply surprised you thought of that before I did. But we don't even know how long she's staying, Ethan. She could decide to just sell the place and leave."

The idea of Summer selling the property and leaving again hits me hard. That had never occurred to me, but Mila's right, as usual. We don't know this Summer, the adult who has a life outside of Dogwood Cove that she might want to go back to. What reason does she even have to stay?

"Still, the apartment beats staying in the motel for however long she is here. It can't hurt to offer it to her," I say, adopting a casual tone.

Mila must buy it because she doesn't call me on my bullshit. "Okay, I was going to text her and tell her to come in tomorrow morning and meet the girls, so I'll mention it to her then."

"Sounds good. I'll talk to you tomorrow. Night Mills."

"Night, big brother."

Putting my phone down on my desk, I turn back to work. The sooner I get everything done, the sooner I can go home, crack a beer, and eat the leftover pizza in my fridge. And try *not* to think too much about Summer Harris.

Right, I don't believe myself when I say that, either.

Chapter 3

Summer

MILA: Come by the bakery whenever you wake up tomorrow and we can catch up!

SUMMER: That sounds great, I'm on Alberta time and wake up pretty early though. What time do you open?

MILA: Girl. I'll be there at 5. Come in whenever you wake up.

SUMMER: Oh. Okay :)

When I push open the door to The Nutty Muffin the next morning, I'm greeted once again by that unmistakable aroma of fresh baking and even better, fresh coffee. Then again, anything beats the gas station coffee I used to buy in Calgary. That stuff tasted like dirty socks and burnt tires. But it was cheap.

I'm so grateful Mila reached out and wanted to get together. But I'm nervous. So nervous that I went back and forth with myself over sending that damn emoji so many times last night, I felt like a complete fool. Twenty years have passed since Mila and I were last together, and I feel like we're starting over. I have never made friends easily, that's why Mila and Ethan were so important to me growing up. Sometimes I think I missed them just as much, if not more than I missed my dad.

"Hey Summer, I'll be right out, pour some coffee and have a seat!" Mila hollers from the back. I grab myself a coffee and settle into one of the big armchairs by the window. Looking out the window at the gazebo in the park across the street, a soft sigh slips past my lips. I have so many memories of town festivals being held there, of playing with Mila and pretending to be princesses. My childhood here was amazing, and I find myself thinking about a future here; maybe someday having my own kids play in that gazebo.

Just as my imagination starts to run wild, Mila waltzes out of the kitchen carrying a plate with what appears to be scones on it. I'm salivating already, and I don't even know what she's offering. One thing is for certain, Mila has turned into one hell of a pastry chef.

"Do you remember when we used to try and use your Easy-Bake Oven to make cupcakes from a recipe instead of that gross mix that came with it?" I say with a grin as I sip my coffee.

Mila groans. "Oh Lord, do I ever. Especially the time we mixed up the salt and the sugar. What a disaster that was." She hands me the plate, and yep, those are some mouthwatering blueberry scones. "Thankfully, my skills have improved since then."

I take a large bite and moan as fresh blueberries and a hint of lemon burst onto my tongue. "They certainly have."

The next few minutes are comfortably quiet as we eat scones and drink coffee.

"I'm really happy you're back." Mila's words pierce the silence and when I look up from my coffee mug, I see her clutching hers. "Don't get me wrong, I wish you were back for a better reason than your dad dying, but it's so good to see you. I want to know everything — all about your life, where you've been, what you're doing. All of it." She gives me an apologetic smile. "Sorry. That was a lot. I'm nervous."

"Me too," I say. "I was so nervous to come here today. I've missed you so much, but it's weird. Right? I mean, a little? I still think of you as my best friend, but I haven't seen you in so long."

Mila stands up and comes in front of me. She drops down to her knees, takes my coffee cup out of my hands and puts it down, then pulls me in for a hug.

"You're back now. Just don't be surprised if I never let you leave again."

I laugh at that. Little does she know, I don't think I *want* to ever leave again.

The tinkle of the bells on the door to the bakery break us apart, and I look over to see two more women walk through.

"My God, Serena Matheson is awake before nine am. It's a freaking miracle!" Mila cries as she walks over to hug the newcomers. I stay in my chair, unsure who these women are. They seem friendly enough, shooting me welcoming but curious glances.

"Yeah, well, you said it was important," the tall blonde who must be Serena answers. She hangs up her coat, then joins the other woman, who's pouring a cup of tea. Mila takes a bite of a scone, and the other two come and sit down beside us. After an awkward moment of silence, all eyes turn to Mila who blinks, looking between the three of us before exclaiming "Oh, right! You don't know each other!"

I have to chuckle at that as Serena simply shakes her head.

"Serena, Paige, this is Summer, my best friend from when we were kids. She's back and I want her to stay forever. Summer, this is Serena and Paige, and we're all going to start a book club." Mila leans back and takes another large bite of her scone. Apparently, that's all the introductions we get.

I wave awkwardly at the two women. "Hi, it's nice to meet you. What's this about a book club?"

Paige pushes her glasses up her nose and sits forward. "Oh yes, that was my idea. I've been doing a lot of investigating into the ways that romance novels actually fight patriarchal societal structures, and when I mentioned my research to Serena and Mila, they decided it would be an enjoyable experience to read a book together and discuss it. We're having our first meeting next week. I can send you the list of discussion questions if you wish. I think they're quite thought provoking."

Well, okay then. Paige's speech is very formal sounding, and I definitely have never heard someone sound so enthusiastic about discussion questions before.

"Paige owns the bookstore next door and is the book nerd of us all. And we love her for it. But hey, Paige, tone it down a bit for us common folk would ya? We just want to read the sexy stuff," Serena teases, nudging her friend. Then she turns back to Mila and crosses her arms. "Not that it isn't lovely to meet Summer." She tosses a warm smile my way. "Because it is, but why the heck did I have to get up so freaking early for this?"

Paige leans toward me conspiratorially. "Serena is not a morning person."

She doesn't seem offended by the book nerd's comment at all, so I smile at her and whisper, "I can see that."

"Sue me for wanting my friends to all meet at a time when I'm not knee-deep in customers."

My attention is drawn back to the discussion between Serena and Mila. Although bickering is more what's happening, not discussing. Mila's rolling her eyes and Serena's narrowing hers.

"Fine. But if I'm going to be up this early, I need a cinnamon bun."

"I made scones."

"Cinnamon bun."

Mila huffs out a dramatic sigh. "Fine. God, you're so demanding. Go and get your damn cinnamon bun from the kitchen, Serena, and while you're up, pour a cup of coffee. Herbal tea is clearly not enough for your grumpy mood right now." Mila says, fixing Serena with a pointed look.

Serena stands up, her hands going to her hips. "I don't drink caffeine. It's poison." She turns and stalks toward the kitchen, as Mila gets in one last shot.

"Sugar is worse than caffeine!"

Serena turns and sticks her tongue out at Mila, and I suppress a giggle. I can tell already that these women are good friends. Being welcomed by them feels so good and having more friends in town than just Ethan and Mila is going to make living here while I figure out what to do with the resort a lot more fun.

At the thought of Ethan, my cheeks grow warm. I wouldn't mind him being more than just a friend. But that's one train of thought that I need to shut down, quickly. Especially in front of Mila. With so many years separating us, I don't exactly know how she'll respond to the news that I'm attracted to her brother.

"If you want to come to the store after this, I'll get you a copy of the book and the discussion questions," Paige says.

"Huh? What?" I say, my brain taking a moment to switch from my pesky attraction to Ethan to books.

"Book club?" She raises her eyebrows.

"Oh, right. Book club. Thanks." Paige nods, satisfied with my rushed response, I guess.

"So, when are you going to reopen Oceanside?" Serena asks when she's back with her cinnamon bun.

Her question is direct and leaves me stumped as to how to answer. Because the truth is, I don't even know if I *will* reopen Oceanside.

"Oh my God, Serena, give her a break, she just got into town yesterday." Mila smacks Serena lightly on the arm.

"Oww, I didn't mean anything bad, I'm just curious. Last time I drove down there to take a look, the place was a dump. I can't imagine how much cash it'll take to fix it up." Serena rubs her arm, glowering at Mila before turning to me with an apologetic expression on her face.

"Sorry, Summer. No offense intended, I'm sure you've got everything figured out."

"Actually, I don't have a fucking clue what to do," I blurt out, hating the frantic tone of my voice. Mila stands up and comes to sit on the arm of my chair, wrapping her arm around my shoulder and resting her head on mine.

"How can we help?"

"Got any big piles of money lying around? Or a job? Or a place to live?" I hate how my voice cracks when I ask. I laugh, but it comes out sounding hollow, and apparent that my attempt to make it seem like I'm joking didn't work.

"Actually," Mila says, lifting her head off of mine and grinning at me, "I do have an apartment you can use."

My jaw drops. "Really?"

"Yeah, it's right above the bakery. Ethan and I own this whole building, and that apartment has been vacant for a month. It's just a small studio, but it's yours if you want it," Mila says with a smile. "And rent is cheap. First month is free while you get yourself figured out. I'm just happy to hear you say you're staying."

I'm overcome with gratitude, both for the offer of an apartment, and for the easy way Mila has opened her heart to me again.

"Thank you," I manage to get out.

Mila waves her hand as if her saving me a month of motel rates and not charging me rent is no big deal. But it is, it's a huge deal. This is the first time in my adult life that I have someone around who supports me; someone who wants to help me.

"Don't worry about it, that's what friends are for," she says breezily. "Besides, it was Ethan's idea to let you have it."

I have to work quickly to school my reaction to that. Not that I'm surprised Ethan was looking out for me, it's what he used to do when we were kids as well. Always making sure we were safe and happy. But his thoughtfulness causes a different reaction in me now.

"What did you do for work before you came here?" The polite question comes from Paige.

"I was a yoga instructor," I answer, taking a sip of my coffee. "I don't suppose there's a studio in town that might need a new teacher?"

Mila frowns. "Darn, no, the nearest studio is in Westport." Her face brightens. "Ooh, you could open one!"

I smile sadly. "I would love to, but I'm going to be way too busy with the resort." I shift in my seat, wanting to move the conversation away from me and all of my problems. "It's okay, really. I'll figure something out. Enough about my stuff. Mila, you have to tell me how you managed to open a bakery! I thought you were going to open an animal shelter. What happened to that dream?"

Mila bursts out laughing. "Oh God, that's right. I forgot I wanted to do that when I was a kid. Let's just say a few shifts volunteering at the shelter over in Westport was enough to turn me off. All that noise, all that poop, no thanks. I still want to have a bunch of animals some day, just not that many."

We all laugh at that, and the next hour is filled with casual conversation. For a moment I let myself pretend as if I never left Dogwood Cove. As if I have always been friends with these ladies, instead of being the newcomer trying to fit in.

Eventually, Mila's staff arrive and it's time for her to open the bakery. She heads off to get her apron on and start serving customers while the rest of us are putting on our coats.

"I'm going home for a nap before my tot dance class, but it was really great to meet you." Serena pulls me in for a hug.

"You, too. Sorry to make you get up early," I say. She shakes her head and shoots another mock glare at Mila, who's behind the counter assisting a customer.

"Nah, don't apologize. It wasn't you; Mila just lives to drive me nuts. It's probably still payback for the one time, *one time*, I flirted with Ethan when we were all drunk last summer." Serena shrugs, oblivious to the massive weight she has dumped on my shoulders. "She's a little protective of him ever since Aubrey. But seriously, I'm not interested in him, it was the tequila talking."

At my confused expression, Serena gives me a guilty smile. "Oh, right. You have no clue what I'm talking about. Umm, it's not really my business, but the short version is, Ethan got his heart broken by this chick, Aubrey. She came to town a few years ago to teach at the elementary school. Everyone thought they would end up married, but then one day she just up and left. I have no idea why, though. Mila and Ethan don't talk about her anymore. Anyway, I'm outta here. See you around, Summer!"

I watch Serena leave, frozen in place by everything she just revealed. Ethan had his heart broken and Mila doesn't like her friends flirting with him. Now I *really* don't want to let on that I'm attracted to him.

"Come on, let's get you the book and discussion questions for book club so you're prepared."

Paige's voice penetrates my wandering thoughts, bringing me back to the present.

We put on our coats, wave to Mila, and then leave together. Next door to the café, she unlocks a purple door that says *Pages* on it, with *Bibliophiles Welcome* in smaller script underneath. The name makes me snort quietly; trust Paige to name a store after herself. She strikes me as the subtly funny type.

The interior is dim without the lights on, but clean. I can see rows and rows of bookshelves, but it doesn't feel crowded. Quirky décor and comfy furniture dot the area, giving the whole store a cozy, welcoming atmosphere. Paige makes a beeline straight for one shelf and pulls a book down immediately. Then she marches over to a curtained-off area marked *Office* and comes back a moment later to hand me the book that is in her hands.

"Here's the book, the questions are inside the front cover. We're meeting next week at my house." she says, very matter-of-fact. I like that about her, she's very concise with her words.

"Thanks, Paige," I say, and I mean it. The way these women have welcomed me so quickly is baffling to someone who has struggled to make meaningful friendships her entire adult life.

"Hey shorty, hey Paige." Ethan strolls up to us, his hands in the front pockets of his jeans. He's wearing another plaid shirt, this one blue and grey, unbuttoned over a white T-shirt, and I can see the outline of his pecs underneath. He's not wearing a hat today, and the thick waves of his brown hair are screaming at me to run my fingers through them, to try and tame the messy, tousled look he's got going on. The look that makes me imagine him first thing in the morning, lying in bed.

"Hi Ethan, can I help you find a book today?" Paige asks. Apparently, she can't sense that I'm spinning off into fantasyland just from being this close to him, smelling him, seeing him. It's more than a little awkward feeling this way about the guy I used to play tag with as a kid.

"No thanks, Paige. I was actually here for Summer." Ethan turns to me, and his megawatt smile blinds me. "Mila mentioned she told you about the apartment, so I wondered if you wanted to go on a little walk around town to reacquaint you with the place."

"Oh that's...you don't..." I huff out a breath, hating how I'm fumbling my words. Ethan stands there, smiling, while Paige is looking at me as if I've sprouted a second head.

"Just say, thanks, Ethan that would be great," he teases.

"Thanks, Ethan that would be great," I mumble back.

His answering laugh sends a thrill right through me, but when he puts his hand on my lower back to escort me out of the store, I feel his touch like a brand on my soul. I had another dream last night of my dad and the man holding my hand. This time, even though I couldn't see the man's face, my subconscious mind somehow decided that man was Ethan. Which makes this even more awkward because suddenly I'm envisioning holding Ethan's hand in real life.

I am in so much trouble.

Chapter 4

Ethan

I try not to smile too widely at how adorably nervous Summer seems, but it does make me stand up a little taller to see that she seems just as flustered by me as I am by her. I caught her staring when I walked into the bookstore, and it took all my strength not to stare right back. She's so fucking beautiful, I froze for a second when I first saw her through the window.

We walk out of Paige's store, and when I have to drop my hand from her back, I swear I see her shoulders drop. But seeing as she's still my little sister's friend, and I have no idea how long she plans on being in town, it's probably for the best that I try and maintain a little distance.

"Not much has changed since you were here, honestly," I start conversationally as we cross the street to the park that's in the center of town. We climb up the steps of the gazebo, and I see that it'll need a fresh coat of paint this summer. That will be the perfect project for some high school kids looking for extra credit, and

I make a mental note to send an email to the principal later.

I walk over to one side and lean against the railing, putting a little distance between Summer and I. Honestly, I don't trust my body's reaction if I'm close to her.

"Mr. Reynolds sold the Grab N' Go several years ago, but the couple that runs it now kept it mostly the same," I say, gesturing to the grocery store that takes up one large building. "The elementary school got some much needed upgrades, but the older kids still have to bus out of town to Westport."

Summer wanders over and stands beside me. "It's still so relaxed here. Everyone seems happy."

I nod. "For the most part, we are."

"Do your parents still live in the house on Cherry Lane?"

The familiar pang of sadness at any mention of my parents hits me.

"No, they don't." She turns to me, waiting for me to go on. Oh crap. It's been so long since I had to tell someone about my parents. I run my hand through my hair, glancing down at the ground because I know if I see her face it'll kill me.

"Shit, Summer, this is hard to tell you. Mom and Dad died in a car accident six years ago." The familiar pang of grief hits me but fades quickly. Every time I think about them, it gets a little easier.

Her gasp of dismay crashes into me. Then she throws her arms around my waist and holds me tightly.

"I'm so sorry, Ethan."

"Hey, it's okay. They went quickly and they went together."

She pulls back and her palm comes to land on my chest. She looks up at me with sorrow in her eyes.

"Still, I wish I had known, I should've been here for you and Mila. I missed so much."

I guide her over to the bench and we sit down. I only wish I knew what else to do or say to make her feel better, but the truth is, grief is a bitch. I've worked my way through all the stages ever since losing my parents, but that doesn't make it any easier. After a few minutes of silence, Summer slaps her hands down on her legs, then stands up.

"Ready to show me some more?"

I nod, and we walk down the steps on the opposite side of the gazebo and cross the street in front of city hall.

"What happened to Mayor De Costa? Did she finally retire?" Summer asks.

"Yeah, she did. Not long after you left. There's been a few others since then, and well, I'm the mayor now." I put my hands in my pockets, feeling a sense of pride at my admission.

"How did *that* happen? There's a lightness back in her voice that fills me with relief. Now this is a story I don't mind sharing.

"My buddy Reid is to blame for that."

"Reid Corser? He's still around?"

"Yeah, he's a lifer just like Mila and I. He's the principal at the elementary school now. When our last mayor, Betty Chow, announced her retirement, no one stepped forward to run as her replacement. Reid suckered me into it, spinning some ridiculous tale of outside influences ruining the town if no one local ran. It took a couple of beers to get me to agree, but eventually I did. That was three years ago, and no one's kicked me out of office yet." I shrug, but the truth is, it feels good to be trusted by everyone to run the town. I might not always love the job, but I do love the town.

"Wow," Summer says, sounding impressed. "Mayor Monroe has a nice ring to it." She turns around to look back at city hall, which we passed a few minutes ago. "So your office is in there?"

I nod.

"Fancy," she says teasingly. "I'll have to come and visit you at work one day. Watch you acting all Mayorish."

Suddenly, visions of Summer bent over my desk fill my mind with dirty ideas. I shut down that train of thought as fast as I can, but then her hand comes up to rest on my shoulder and I swear I feel a shock of connection run through me.

"Is Sweet Scoops still open? I know it's still morning, but I could go for some butter pecan ice cream right about now."

That makes me chuckle. "I forgot about your crazy sweet tooth. Come on, consider it my welcome back treat."

"Need any help moving your stuff over from the motel?" I ask as we walk out of Sweet Scoops a little while later, bowls of ice cream in hand. "I just have to get the key for the apartment from my house."

"I don't have much," she says.

That makes me pause. It does seem odd that she was able to pick up and move here so easily, and hearing she doesn't have a lot of stuff to deal with makes me curious to find out more about her past and soon.

"Right. Yeah. Well, why don't I meet you back at the bakery later instead, so I can let you in. I'm happy to help you get settled." I know I'm sounding desperate, and I can't bring myself to care. I need more time with her.

"Ethan!"

Before Summer answers me, my buddy Reid comes jogging up the street. It's like he knew we were just talking about him...I watch his eyes widen as he takes in Summer standing beside me and I fight back a wave of possessiveness that comes over me. It's clear he doesn't recognize her, and it's clear he's noticed how beautiful she is.

"What's up, Reid?" I grind out, glaring at him, trying to say without words that he needs to back off. But he doesn't get the message, judging by the grin on his face.

"Reid Corser, and you are?" He sticks his hand out toward Summer, completely ignoring me.

"Hey, Reid. It's me, Summer. I grew up here, remember?" she says, shaking his hand with a small laugh.

"Holy shit, Summer Harris? I heard you were back in town!"

My blood pressure skyrockets as Reid leans over and hugs Summer. Her arms go around his waist, and I'm seeing red. Or is it green? I blink away my consuming jealousy, fully aware that it's insane to feel this way over a woman who isn't even mine, just in time to hear Reid seal his own fate. He's a dead man.

"Why don't we get dinner together tomorrow, and I can catch you up on all the town gossip."

"Dude, she just got here, give it a minute, would you?" I grumble, snatching Summer's arm and tugging her back to my side as my eyes shoot daggers at my friend. Reid startles and finally looks at me. Recognition dawns on his face, and he takes a step back, smirking at me.

"Right. Of course, man. My bad." He turns to Summer, who seems confused by my behaviour. I guess I don't blame her. "I'm sure I'll see you around, Summer. Good to have you back."

With a slap to my back, he continues on jogging down the street and my rage lowers from *kill him now*, to *shit I've made a fool of myself* level.

I drop Summer's arm and stuff my hands in my pockets, my gaze not leaving the ground as Summer stands silently in front of me.

"So that was weird," she blurts out, and I outwardly wince. "What was the caveman routine all about?"

"I'm sorry," I mumble, and out of the corner of my eye I notice she steps closer, and her hand lifts to cup my chin firmly, forcing my gaze upward.

"Ethan. Talk to me."

"It's nothing. Sorry. I just figured you might want some time to get settled." My reason sounds lame even to me, but Summer seems to drop it. Thank God, because that could have been awkward. "Anyway, I guess I'll leave the key with Mila. I just remembered a meeting I'm late for."

Then, before I can say or do anything else stupid, I turn and walk away.

That night I sleep like shit. I can't stop tossing and turning, my semiconscious mind swirling with confusing images of Summer. Sometimes she's a kid, playing and laughing with Mila, and sometimes we're adults, running along the beach and holding hands. Then it goes dark, and when my vision clears, she's in her truck driving away from me.

People always leave.

The problem is, I don't think I could handle Summer Harris leaving again.

Two days pass and I'm even more confused by my reaction to Summer being back in town. Tonight she and Mila are coming over for dinner, and it will be the first time I've seen her since the day we walked around town. I still don't know what to do about the fact that I'm attracted to her. Part of me wants to forget about it and force those feelings away. She needs a friend more than anything else right now. But another part of me can't quite ignore the pull I feel toward her. It's more than friendship, and I want to know if it goes both ways.

"Ethan?" Mila calls out as she pushes open my front door without knocking. I left it unlocked, knowing she would do just that.

"In the kitchen," I reply, keeping my attention on the avocado I'm cutting for guacamole.

"Holy shit, big brother, you have *candles?*" Mila says as she walks into the room, Summer following behind. I glare at my sister. Of course she had to notice the goddamn candles I dug out of the closet. I don't remember buying them, and given the layer of dust on the box I found them in means my mom probably did at some point.

Ignoring her comment, I smile at Summer. "Hey, ladies. Help yourself to a drink, I've got beer and wine in the fridge."

"What? You never have wine for me." Mila whines, and I shoot her another look that she misses completely.

"Yeah, well, tonight I do."

Summer wanders over to stand beside me, her delicate peppermint and lavender scent wafting up from the top of her head. I try not to be too obvious as I inhale deeply.

She sneaks a piece of avocado, looking up at me, her eyes dancing. "Thanks, I'm good with beer." She winks, then twirls around to Mila who is pouring a glass of wine.

They wander into my living room and I follow, chips and guac in hand. Setting it down on the table, I go back to the kitchen and get a beer for myself before joining them.

Mila's got her legs draped over the arm of my favourite chair, leaving the spot next to Summer on the couch as the only open seat.

I let the girls carry the conversation, but when the topic turns to the book Paige chose for the book club they're apparently starting, I take that as my time to leave. I make my way into the kitchen and finish some final things for dinner. The sound of Summer's laugh at something Mila said makes me smile.

"Dinner is served," I call out to them.

"This looks amazing, Ethan," Summer says appreciatively.

"He's an awesome cook. But leave the baking to me." Mila piles two tacos onto a plate and hands it over to Summer before filling her own. We sit down and for the next few minutes the only sounds are of us eating.

"So, I was thinking, why don't we organize a work party to help cleanup Oceanside?"

Summer's eyes widen at Mila's suggestion and I think she's a little overwhelmed by the offer.

"Oh, umm, wow. You really think people would do that? Come and help me?"

I lightly touch the back of her hand, briefly. "Of course they would, Summer. The town wants to see the resort opened again. We all cared about your dad, and you."

She looks at me silently, but her expressive eyes show a display of emotion. "Thank you. That means a lot, more than you know."

Mila stands up and goes to give her a hug around the shoulders. "We're going to make that place amazing, just like your dad wanted."

I nod in agreement, and raise my beer. "To renovating Oceanside."

We all clink our drinks together, then turn our attention back to the food. After, we sit around the table, talking about the work that needs to be done at the resort. Eventually, Mila's yawning grows more frequent, and the girls stand up to leave. I make sure to hug Mila first, and when it comes to Summer, I try to keep it casual. But she feels so goddamn good in my arms, it's hard to resist holding her a little bit longer.

"Summer, you have to come with us to the beach tomorrow," Mila says, pulling Summer out of my arms.

She turns to me next. "You're coming, too, right? You and Reid are in charge of the bonfire."

"Yeah, I'm coming."

"Great, we can all carpool." As usual, my bulldozer of a sister is making plans for everyone.

"Won't the water be freezing?" Summer asks with a laugh. Man, that laugh.

"We aren't going swimming, silly! But we can take the kayaks down and paddle around if we want, or just hang out around the fire. C'mon, it'll be fun. The girls will be there, too." Mila wheedles, and I chance a glance at Summer to see her reaction.

She's smiling.

"Okay, I'll come."

Chapter 5

Summer

Mila insisted we drive together to the beach, but what she didn't tell me was that Ethan would be the one driving both of us. Sitting in the front seat of his truck next to him, with Mila in the backseat, feels good. Too good. As if I never left and we're still the three friends we were as kids. With only two years between us, we played together a lot.

"Oh my God, do you remember the time Ethan caught us trying on Mom's bras?"

Mila's been reminiscing about our childhood the entire drive. So far, the stories have been cute and fun to remember, but this story is not one I really want to revisit.

"Mila..." I start, but she ignores me.

"We had to hold them on our flat as a pancake chest, but damn, we thought we looked so grown up!" She dissolves into a fit of giggles.

I close my eyes to hide my dismay that she chooses *that* story to bring up. I know she isn't trying to embarrass me. To her, this is nothing more than three friends sharing stories about their childhood. But given how my perception of Ethan has changed from friend to handsome man I would like to kiss, I'd really rather we not go into any more mortifying stories from when I was a kid and he saw me almost naked.

Ethan's low chuckle sends shivers down my spine, in spite of my embarrassment. When I chance a quick glance over at him, he seems relaxed and completely at ease, one arm propped on the console between us, the other resting easily on the steering wheel. He's wearing a ball cap again today, and maybe on a different guy it would look immature, but on him it's damn sexy. No plaid, just a T-shirt, thanks to the surprisingly warm spring day we're having. It's perfect beach weather. *Maybe he'll take his shirt off...*I stifle a groan at that mental image in time to catch the tail end of another story from Mila, this one thankfully about herself and not me.

"I can't believe the shit we used to do as such young kids. The freedom we had," Mila sighs. "That's why someday I want to raise my family right here in Dogwood Cove. I want them to have the freedom and fun we did."

"And where, exactly, is this family coming from? Last time I checked you were flying solo. Anyone I need to beat up?" Brotherly teasing and affection come out in Ethan's words, and Mila reaches in front to smack him lightly in response.

"A girl can dream, okay? Besides, I'm not the only one in this truck with no love life." I see her stick her tongue out at him in the rearview mirror and based on the smirk Ethan gives in return, he saw it, too. Mila turns to me, and I know what's coming next before she even opens her mouth. "What about you, Summer? Anyone special in Calgary?"

I swear I see Ethan's gaze flash to mine, wide with curiosity before he returns to watching the road. And I know I see his hands tighten on the steering wheel, both of them holding on rigidly now. Interesting.

"No, no one special," I say softly, trying to watch him out of the corner of my eye. He relaxes; it's subtle, but I see it.

"Well, I hate to be the bearer of bad news, but Dogwood Cove has a serious lack of hot, single men," Mila says dramatically.

"Hey, what am I, if not a hot, single man?"

My heart skips a beat at Ethan's words, laced with innuendo. But Mila is oblivious to it.

"Eww. Ethan, stop. You're family. You don't count."

I risk one more look over at him, and this time I catch him glancing back at me. It's the tiny upward turn of his lips in the barest hint of a smile that makes my heart speed up, however.

When we get to the public beach, over on the other side of town from where Oceanside is located, there's quite a few vehicles in the parking lot. Ethan reaches into the bed of his truck and hands Mila a blanket, then she's gone, skipping down to the beach, leaving the two of us alone.

"Mills is so happy you're back."

He says it so quietly, I almost don't hear him.

"You still call her Mills? I thought she hated that." I smile.

He chuckles, and the sound washes over me like warm, melted chocolate. "Why do you think I do it?"

I laugh as well, so content in this moment with him that I almost forget everyone who's waiting for us. Before I can second-guess myself, I blurt out "Are you happy I'm back?"

His eyes darken, and the way he is staring at me so intently, it could light a fire with its heat. "Of course I am." His hand lifts up as if he's going to touch me, and I hold my breath in anticipation, but then he lets it drop back down to his side.

My breath escapes in a loud whoosh, and I turn away from him to try and control my reaction. Holy crap on a cracker, he's potent.

"You want to take the drinks cooler, or the bag with towels and stuff?"

When I look back, his eyes are normal again, as if he hadn't been stripping me bare with his gaze seconds earlier.

"Bag, please," I manage to croak out, before taking the bag and following Mila's path at a near jog. Space. I need space. Because, wow.

When I reach Mila, she already has one blanket spread out, lining up with several others. Serena, Paige, and Reid are all spread out, chatting with each other. I put down my load, suddenly feeling awkward. Everyone has been friends for so long, and even though they have been nothing but welcoming, it's hard not to feel like an outsider.

"Hey, Summer!" Reid calls out when he sees me, giving me a wide smile. I wonder if Mila or any of the girls have ever dated him. When she said there were no hot guys in Dogwood Cove, she didn't mention him.

"Hey, guys," comes a low rumble of a voice before I can respond to Reid. I can feel the heat of Ethan's body standing close behind me. He must have walked up without me even realizing it. I wave awkwardly, and everyone goes back to their conversation as I sit down on the blanket beside Mila, resolutely not meeting Ethan's gaze. I don't know how to feel about the pull I can sense between us now. The easy friendship is there, the same as when we were younger. But now it's layered with something else, something far more powerful. And I'm not sure I'm ready to figure out what that is.

I haven't had a day like this in forever. Mila convinces me to go kayaking with her, and we spend an hour on the water, watching for seals. I missed the ocean living in Alberta, and it is so invigorating to be by the water again. When we pull the boats up to the beach, Ethan comes to help, and when our hands brush, I swear I feel a spark of something undefinable in that casual touch.

Reid brought a portable grill, so while he cooks burgers, the rest of us play volleyball for a while. Then, after lunch, the girls and I go for a walk along the beach while Ethan and Reid take the kayaks out.

"One of the dance moms asked me yesterday if I would teach adult classes," Serena says as we walk slowly down the beach. "She specifically wanted to know if I could teach *pole dancing* classes." She shudders delicately. "I'm a freaking ballerina, not a stripper!"

"Pole dancing is meant to be a killer workout. I'd sign up," Mila says, stooping to pick up a shell.

"And strippers work incredibly hard. I'm not knocking them; I'm only saying that's a little out of my comfort zone." Serena replies, shrugging her shoulders. "But I have been thinking of offering some adult classes. Just not sure what. The idea of having to teach the dance moms isn't high on my list of things I want to do."

"I could probably come up with some yoga classes that would make them happy, if you're interested in that," I offer.

Serena claps her hands and spins around in excitement. "Oh my God, yes! I was half asleep that morning at the bakery, but now I totally remember you telling us you were an instructor. That's perfect. We need to find a time to work out the details, soon, so I can get those dance moms off my back."

"That's such a good idea," Mila chimes in. "You realize, you're never getting out of here again, right?" She threads her arm through mine, pulling me in close.

I lean my head down on her shoulder, letting the warmth of friendship seep through me. "Sounds good to me."

Eventually we make our way back to the blankets where the guys are relaxing with a beer, laughing about who won the race they apparently had on the water. Reid passes me a beer and gestures for me to sit down next to him.

"What do you think of the town? Has it changed much since you left?"

His question is harmless, but across from us I see Ethan's gaze narrow as he takes in the sight of Reid and I sitting side by side. What the heck is that all about? I frown slightly, wondering if there's some chance that Ethan is jealous of Reid. But I quickly dismiss the notion. There might be something weird brewing between us, but at the end of the day, Ethan and I are nothing more than friends. Besides, I have zero interest in Reid, and aside from that first day when he asked me to dinner, Reid hasn't shown any interest in me, either.

"Not much, but to be honest, I'm not sure as a child I was really paying close attention to the town. Looking at it now, it's got some definite Stars Hollow vibes," I say with a chuckle.

"Does that make Ethan our version of Taylor Doose?" Mila calls out as she drops down beside her brother.

"Who the hell is Taylor Doose?" Ethan retorts, raising an eyebrow at his sister.

Mila rolls her eyes and shoves him with her shoulder. "Only the most underappreciated character on *Gilmore Girls*, that's who."

"Tell the truth, Mila, Taylor is a grumpy stick-in-the-mud who's always sticking his nose in other people's business," Serena chimes in.

"Exactly, so…Ethan." Mila says triumphantly and everyone laughs, including me. Ethan just shakes his head good-naturedly and eventually the conversation turns to something else.

It's been as close to a perfect day as I can remember. Spending time with friends, relaxing, and not worrying about anything. The sunshine, the water, everything about today has filled my soul in so many ways.

I'm truly starting to believe that I am meant to be here, back in Dogwood Cove. After so many years wandering the country, feeling lost and untethered because of the nomad lifestyle my mother dragged me into, it's nice to find some roots again.

And later, when the sun starts to set, we move the blankets around and set up a big fire ring. Ethan and Reid carry loads of firewood down from the truck, and soon we've got a bonfire going. Sitting around the fire, surrounded by friends, I'm living a scene from a movie. Ethan walks over to where I'm sitting, and before he drops to the blanket beside me, he pulls out a couple of small packets of something and gives them to me.

"Remember these?"

I look down and gasp. "Magic flame? You found magic flame?"

Memories of bonfires when we were kids come flooding back. How entranced we would be when Mila and Ethan's parents would scatter the packages of various chemicals on the fire, making the flames dance in all different colours.

"I remembered how much you loved them," he answers gruffly.

I turn to him, my heart brimming with emotion. "Thank you."

"Told you I'm glad you're back."

So am I.

Chapter 6

Ethan

Our day at the beach was a few days ago, and since then I haven't been able to stop thinking about Summer. So naturally, when my evening run takes me past the playground at the elementary school and I see her sitting on the swings all alone, my footsteps slow down and turn in her direction without a second thought. It's dusk and the school grounds are empty, the kids and teachers all gone home. Fleetingly I wonder if Reid was out here talking to her after finishing his day as principal, but I dismiss that thought quickly. Even if I never act on my attraction to Summer, I know he would never make a move.

When I get close to her, I frown. She's been crying again. The Summer I remember as a child was tough, rarely cried, and was happy almost all the time. I know she has had a hell of a lot to deal with lately, but I don't like seeing her sad. I want to comfort her, to make her feel better. I want to take away her sadness and replace it with joy.

"What's up shorty, you need somebody to push you?" I keep my tone light and teasing as I walk up to her, trying not to make it obvious that I can see she's upset. She smiles at me brightly, one hand brushing away her tears.

"Hey Ethan, what are you doing here?"

I gesture to my clothes and shoes. "Out for a run, saw you here all by yourself, figured I'd see if you want some company."

Summer looks around, her head resting on the metal chain of the swing. "I was walking around, checking out the rest of the town, and I found myself here." She pushes off with her feet, slowly moving back and forth. I stay standing to the side, my arms resting loosely crossed in front of my chest. "I loved this school. Mr. Wagner, our grade two teacher, he used to wear silly costumes all the time. A lab coat and pretend mustache for science, giant glasses and a bow tie for math; he made it so fun. And Mrs. Song, the librarian, she always had the perfect book for each of us to read. Somehow, she always knew what we wanted each week. And this playground..."

Her voice trails off, and I can tell she's lost in the memories of her childhood. I let myself go there, too, only every memory has Summer in it. Which is weird, because we didn't actually spend that much time together as kids. But I can remember her and Mila jumping in piles of leaves that my dad and I spent hours raking, and a lot of times the three of us plus Reid would ride our bikes to the corner store for candy and ice cream. After school, I would be in charge of walking the girls home. But we were allowed to stay and play at this very playground for a while before we had to be home, and most of the time I would be roped into a game of tag or hide and seek with Mila and Summer. Sure, there were some days when I felt too old to be playing silly games with little girls, but most of the time I was fine with it. We had fun.

"Did you stay in touch with my dad?" She sounds nervous, almost as if she's not sure she wants to hear my answer.

"Yeah," I say gruffly. "Mom and Dad would invite him over for dinner every now and then."

"Did he…did he ever talk about me?"

Fuck. This sucks. She's in pain, and I'm about to make it worse.

"Not to us. And Mom and Dad told us not to bring you up around him, no matter how much Mila wanted to ask him. It killed her that you left and we never heard from you again. She wanted to know why, but our parents figured it would only hurt your dad to talk about you."

Summer is silent and still. I can't stand it anymore, so I walk behind her and put my hands on the chain of the swing, pulling her back gently. She looks over her shoulder, and I see a ghost of a smile lift her lips just before I push her away from me. For several minutes we don't talk, I simply push her on the swing as she goes higher and higher. Her hair is flying out behind her, and eventually I hear her laugh, and the weight on my heart lightens. I make my way to the swing next to her and sit down, kicking my feet lightly so I move back and forth a little. Her eyes are closed, so I can watch her without wondering if she'll notice. Her face is upturned to the dusky sky, and she's smiling. She's so fucking beautiful, I wonder what she would feel like under my touch, whether her skin would be soft under my kisses. Just those fleeting thoughts are enough to make my dick stir in my shorts and I have to think of something else to distract myself before it becomes apparent.

Dirty underwear... cleaning toilets...

Eventually her swing slows down until she's beside me, but since we're facing each other, it's easy to meet her gaze.

"Can you tell me about him?"

I wish my parents were still alive. They would have so many more stories to tell her, not to mention they would be so happy she's back. In that sense, I guess Summer and I have something in common beyond our childhood friendship. We've both lost a parent; the difference is I had most of my life with mine, but she was taken away from hers long before he actually died. She can never get those missing years back. I do have one story I can share with her that I hope makes her smile.

"He stayed involved with the town, kept on delivering the mail right up until retiring at sixty. When I took over as mayor, he showed up at my office one day in November and handed me a red and white striped pen." I chuckle at the memory of Carl standing in my office with a very stern expression on his face, me behind my desk, scared to death about the job I was unprepared for.

"He said to me, 'Mayor Monroe, I'm here to tell you a part of your job no one ever talks about. You, my friend, are now Santa Claus.'"

Summer giggles. "What? That makes no sense!"

"Ah, but it does. See, Canada Post has their letter to Santa program, where if kids write a letter to Santa, someone has to answer it. Normally staff at one of the main branches would take care of it, but for some reason, out here, the job used to fall on your dad. I guess a few years before I took over, he approached Mayor Chow about getting some help with it, and she volunteered to take it on. Except, when I succeeded her as mayor, she neglected to tell me that. It wasn't until your dad showed up with that damn pen that I knew what I was in for. I signed two hundred and something letters that first year."

"Oh, Ethan, that's adorable!" Her eyes are shining again, not with tears, but with happiness. Damn does that make me feel good.

"Yeah, he took that and other things really seriously. Especially when it came to the kids in town. Every fall he would have mini chocolate bars in his mailbag for about a week leading up to Halloween, and if he saw a kid while he was out on his route he'd call out 'trick or treat' to them and toss them a candy." I shake my head at that memory, smiling at the reaction from Reid's ex-girlfriend Sasha one year, who was horrified that kids would accept candy from what she figured was a stranger. "Everyone knew him and loved him. The town took care of him when your mom took you away. And when he died, we all mourned him."

"I wish I was here for that. I wish I knew him like that. When I left, I had no idea I would never see him again."

When I look over at her, Summer's hands are clenched so tightly on the swing that her knuckles are white. Her brow is furrowed, and her cheeks are flushed. Even angry and hurting, she's still so stunning it takes my breath away.

"Why didn't you come back sooner?" The question escapes me before I can think about how it might sound, and even though I worry she'll be mad that I asked, I want to know the answer. That's bugged me since she returned. She doesn't answer me right away. Instead, she stares down at the ground, her feet kicking the wood chips underneath our feet.

"My mom never had a good thing to say about Dogwood Cove. Over and over again she would tell me how awful it was here, how much she hated living here, and how miserable it was. At first she didn't bring my Dad into it, but when I started asking when he was going to join us wherever we were, she told me he didn't want to leave. She made me believe that he didn't want me. It hurt, so badly, but I had no reason to doubt her. Then when I got old enough to realize she didn't exactly care that much about me, either, I was mad at him. Because if she lied to me, and he really did want me, then why didn't he fight? Why didn't he come for me?"

Her voice is full of so much confusion, so much anger and pain. I wish I had the answers that she deserves. Instead, I do the only thing I can do. Offer comfort. I stand up from my swing, take the two steps that put me in front of her, and pull her up and into my arms for a hug. Tentatively I reach my hand up to cup her cheek, and the sensation of her warm skin against my palm almost does me in.

"Your mom lied to you, and from what I can guess, didn't exactly give you a good childhood after you left here. She had no right to keep you from your dad. I don't know why he never went after you, because from what I knew of him, he would have wanted you. Desperately."

"Thank you."

Those two words come out as a watery whisper, and the way she turns her cheek into my palm makes my heart expand with my desire to protect her from pain.

I don't know how much longer I'm going to be able to deny the truth. I want Summer Harris to be more than just my friend.

Chapter 7

Summer

"Get...out...you...mother...truckin'...*weed!*" I yell as my shovel finally breaks loose the gigantic root mass of the bush I'm trying to dig out. Turns out feeling overwhelmed with confusing emotions makes pretty good fuel for hard physical labor. And after that evening at the playground with Ethan, finding out about my dad and everything I missed, well, I've got plenty of emotions built up. In only a couple of hours, I've managed to cleanup most of the weeds and trash around the main building. If Mila really does manage to coordinate a work party, that could take care of most of the cabin cleanup, and then I can properly assess what needs to be done to make this place operational again.

Not that I've got the funds to do any of it, that is. Even if I start teaching classes at Serena's studio, , I won't be able to save much for renovation costs. I'm not afraid to do hard work myself, but even I know this is more than I can handle on my own. Not to mention the cost of tools, supplies, and eventually furniture. The costs keep mounting up in my mind.

I could sell.

It's not the first time this week that the idea has crossed my mind. Sell the property and take the money to help figure out my life. But then I think of letting go of the one connection I have left to my dad, and I know I can't go through with it. I need to make his plans a reality, for him and for me.

I lean the shovel against the side of the building and walk over to the water bottle I set down on the ground. I take a long drink as I watch the waves come into the shore. The ocean has always settled my soul and today is no exception. There is something about the relentless nature of the tide, the way it never gives up its pursuit of the shoreline that gets to me. The waves don't care about material things. They will keep coming whether I clean this place up or not. They are constant.

I want to be constant. I want to be here, rooted in this town that feels like home, in this property that reminds me of my dad, despite the fact we don't have any memories of being here together. He bought it with me in mind, and I will not let him down.

Renewed with fresh energy, I stand up and walk over to the first cabin. I need a break from weed pulling, and my next priority is getting started on cabin cleanup. So far, I've managed to get almost everything out and into a large pile beside the cabin; I'll need Ethan to help me figure out how to take all the garbage to the landfill later. Grabbing a broom and a headlamp so I can see what I'm doing, I push open the door. Getting electricity out here is also a priority, and I add a generator to my running list of expenses that I'll have to face sooner rather than later.

An old shelf hangs from the wall by only one bracket, and I decide to start there. Summoning my strength, I grab hold and pull sharply. It comes away from the wall easily, too easily, as I stumble backwards, dropping it.

"Oww, crap!" I cry, looking down to see a jagged cut in my pants. I hobble outside, sit down on the steps of the cabin, and roll up my pant leg to see a trail of blood coming from a long cut.

"Ouch, ouch, ouch, ouch, ouch." Goddamn it stings, and I hate blood.

"Summer? Shit! What happened?" Ethan's voice is frantic and I lift my eyes up to see him running toward me. He crouches down and gingerly takes my leg in his hands. I can see the tendons standing out in his neck as he runs his fingers down my leg.

"This is bad, Summer. What were you doing?" His voice is full of concern and the pain in my leg is eclipsed by the heat coming from his touch.

"I was pulling a shelf off the wall," I say, gesturing to the cabin behind me, "and my hulk strength made it come off easier than I thought it would. It hit my leg on the way down in retaliation."

That makes Ethan smile briefly, but his lips quickly turn down when he looks back at my leg. "I've got a first aid kit in the truck, but if it was a nail that cut you, you should get a tetanus shot." He stands up and goes into the cabin, coming back out with the offending shelf in hand.

"Yeah, see here? I think this nail caught you. I'll bandage up your leg and take you into town to see Doc. And next time you fight a shelf off the wall, wear something thicker than leggings, okay?" he says gruffly.

My heart is racing and it's not because of the cut on my leg. It's the way Ethan has taken control of things, all alpha male and hot as ever. I nod mutely and watch him jog over to his truck, where he pulls out a red bag before coming back.

This time he sits down on the step beside me and lifts my leg into his lap. He takes out some wipes and a bandage before looking up at me.

"This might sting," he murmurs softly.

I wince because he's right, the alcohol wipes do sting, and I'm a wimp. I keep my eyes trained on the top of his head as he is bent over my leg, carefully cleaning my cut. He's so gentle, his touch feels more like a caress. When he finishes, he wraps a bandage around my leg and secures it with a piece of tape. Then he glances up at me briefly, his gaze trapping mine as he bends down and presses a soft kiss just above the bandage, making a tiny gasp escape my mouth.

"That'll do for now, but let's get you to Doc." His voice is a low rumble that sends shivers down my spine. He stands up, reaches down, and lifts me straight up and into his arms.

"I can walk, you know," I manage to say, pushing at him gently.

"I know, but this is faster." His long legs cover the short distance to his truck quickly, and he slowly lowers me into my seat.

"Thank you," I say, grabbing his hand in mine. Something is shifting between us; it has been ever since Reid asked me out for dinner. I am starting to think my attraction to Ethan isn't all one-sided, and the way his eyes are burning into mine right now is confirming that.

His hand rests on my leg the entire drive into town and all the way to Doc's office. I feel it there, a heavy, warm weight that excites me and calms me at the same time.

We pull up in front of the same old building that I remember from childhood visits to the doctor, making me smile.

"Does Polly still work for Doc? She had the best lollipops," I say and Ethan chuckles. "Wait, is Doc even working anymore? He must be ancient!"

"He is and he is," Ethan replies. "Doc opened a partnership with another doctor several years back. But we still call the place Doc's. Who knows if he'll ever retire fully, but he only works once or twice a week these days."

"And Polly?"

"Her daughter works the reception now. No more lollipops, sorry."

Ethan comes around and opens my door, but when he goes to lift me down, I shake my head at him.

"I can walk."

He steps back, but still offers his arm, which I take gratefully. I hobble up the steps and into the office that still smells clean and medicinal. An unfamiliar woman is sitting at the desk; this must be Polly's daughter. Ethan guides me to a chair before walking over to her and explaining why we are there.

Shortly, a nurse comes into the waiting area and calls my name. Ethan looks at me questioningly, and I nod. He stands and helps me into the room. Truthfully, my leg isn't actually hurting that badly anymore, but I'm enjoying his attention too much to admit that I don't need his help.

The nurse gets us settled and a few minutes later the door opens and an older woman wearing a white lab coat comes in.

"Hello there, I'm Doctor Wilson. You must be Summer?" She looks at me kindly, then turns a puzzled frown on Ethan. "Mayor Monroe, is there a reason you're in here with Miss Harris instead of waiting outside for her?"

Ethan looks to me, and uncertainty is written across his face.

"I don't mind if he stays," I reply, smiling reassuringly at the doctor. Something changed out at the resort when he took care of my leg. I want him here.

"I cleaned the wound with alcohol wipes, but it was a rusty nail that cut her, so I think she'll need a tetanus booster. I don't think she needs stitches, though," Ethan says, fixing the doctor with an intense stare. I want to tell him to relax and let Doctor Wilson do her job, but I don't think he'd appreciate it.

Doctor Wilson makes a noncommittal sound and looks up and over her glasses at Ethan. "I think I'll make my own decisions on a treatment plan, Mayor Monroe, but thank you for your input."

I have to fight to suppress my giggle at the blush that covers Ethan's face from being put in his place like that. But then Doctor Wilson unwraps the bandage, and I wince when I see it again. He reaches his hand out to me and I grab it, holding tightly.

"No stitches necessary, it's a good thing that it's a jagged cut, as that will heal cleaner than a straight one. But we should do a tetanus booster if it's been more than ten years since you had one." Doctor Wilson casts a sly glance over at Ethan. "It would seem Mayor Monroe does, in fact, know the treatment plan you require."

I do laugh at that and the doctor smiles at me in return. Ethan's hand relaxes its grip on mine, and I feel warm inside knowing he was worried. After I've received my shot and a clean bandage, as well as instructions on recognizing signs of infection, Ethan and I are able to leave the clinic.

"Can you drive me back to the resort so I can get my truck?" I ask as we walk down the steps of the clinic. Ethan looks at me in horror.

"You're not driving, Summer. You need to go home and rest your leg. I'll go with Mila to get your truck later."

"Ethan, I'm fine," I protest.

"No way. I'm driving you home and getting you settled. No arguing, shorty."

With me grumbling the whole way, Ethan drives me home and helps me up the stairs to my apartment. Only once I'm settled on the couch with my leg elevated and a glass of water next to me does he stop hovering. He leans down and for a second I think he's going to kiss me, but then his lips brush the top of my head softly and that's all. He walks to my door and pauses.

"There's a farm market every Tuesday afternoon up in Westport. Do you want to come with me this week?" His tone and his pose are casual, but my heart speeds up all the same. Is he asking me out on a date?

"I'd like that."

"Maybe I'll get you a lollipop. You know, since you didn't get one at Doc's."

I toss a pillow at him, but Ethan just chuckles and dodges it as he closes my front door.

Chapter 8

Ethan

When I pick up Summer to take her to the farm market, I realize the error in my decision. Now I have to drive the half hour to the neighbouring town of Westport trying not to let my body betray my reaction to her, and trying even harder not to let my hand fall to touch her shoulder from where it rests on the back of the seat behind her. She looks like her name, a soft summer morning, in a pale-yellow sweater that hangs off one shoulder and cropped jeans. It's sunny today, which explains the sandals on her feet. She smells amazing, that fresh and floral aroma I am beginning to associate with her filling my nostrils. I want to touch her, to feel that sweater and see if it's as soft as I imagine it is. I want to feel the silk of her skin. I want to kiss the spot on her neck where her sweater drapes down and see if she shivers under my lips.

Let's just say that drive has never been so...hard.

"Ethan, this is incredible," Summer says when we finally make it to the market. Rows of vendors with seasonal produce, baked goods, handmade items, and plants surround us. Music comes from a busker down the way and kids are running around with balloons and bags of popcorn. Summer twirls around, making me grin at her excitement. It's so easy to be with her, to let her joy fill me with my own sense of happiness. I grab her hand, and it feels natural when she threads our fingers together.

"It's not quite the best growing season for produce, but we should be able to find some good stuff," I tell her.

"That's okay, half the fun of markets is the surprise at what you find. It's different every time."

Slowly we meander up one side of the market, taking in all of the vendors that are selling everything from pottery to homemade soaps and lotions. One has artisanal oils and vinegar, and another with craft kombucha. Summer pulls me to a stop, and greets the person standing behind the table lined with bottles of the drink. She chooses two for us to sample and hands me one.

"You've got to try some 'booch," Summer says excitedly as I examine the pink liquid.

"Really? Fermented tea?"

"It's so good for you." She pats my stomach, then freezes, leaving her hand in place. "Good for your gut. Not that you have one, Mr. Lumberjack with a six-pack. I mean your inside gut. You know. Oh my God, I'll stop now." She drops her head down on my chest, which is shaking with my laughter.

"I get it, shorty." When my laughs subside, I take a sip of the fizzy drink. "Hmm. Not bad."

Summer smiles up at me, and I realize I'll do almost anything to see that happen. She pays for two bottles of the kombucha, handing me one as we walk on. At another stall, we sample fresh bread and buy some sandwiches for a late lunch, sitting on a bench to eat. For a while, we're quiet, enjoying our food and people watching.

"This is nice," Summer says quietly. I wrap my arm around her and allow myself to trail my fingers up and down her bare arm. Maybe it's because we aren't in Dogwood Cove where anyone could see us, but it feels easy and right to be affectionate with her. She leans into my touch, as if she wants it just as much as I do.

"It is."

No, it's more than nice. It's fucking perfect. I want more days like this, simply the two of us exploring and spending time together.

"Summer,"

"Ethan,"

We both laugh lightly as we turn to face each other on the bench. God, she's so beautiful. Her hair is loose, cascading over her shoulders. Her face is bare of makeup, but she's still the most stunning woman I've ever seen. And I want her.

"You go first," I say, taking her hands in mine.

Summer's cheeks flush a light pink, and her gaze drops down to her lap and our entwined hands.

"This is weirdly difficult," she starts. My heart clenches involuntarily, and Summer glances up at me quickly and continues. "Not in a bad way. In a 'holy crap I can't believe it' way."

"Summer, I'm getting confused," I say gently. But inside my heart is beating wildly as I let myself start to hope that she's going to say she wants the same thing I do.

"Sorry. It's just, you're, well, you're you. Ethan Monroe, Mila's big brother. And now you're also Ethan Monroe, man I'm ridiculously attracted to. And we're touching, and hugging, and it doesn't feel like we're just friends. It's weird, is all, and I don't know what to do about it," she finishes, biting her lip and looking at me.

I act on instinct, leaning in and kissing her lightly. Then her mouth opens with a tiny gasp, and I let go of her hands to cup her face, pulling her in closer. Our lips fuse together, fitting like they were designed for this. I force my hands to stay where they are, instead of traveling her body like I want them to. That will have to wait until we're alone.

"Your mouth feels like heaven," I murmur against her lips, and the corners of hers tip up in response. Her fingers come up to tangle in the hair at the back of my neck, and the way she's holding me to her is possessive and perfect. She wants this just as much as I do. She pulls my face back to hers and I lose track of time and all awareness of anything around us as I kiss her. She tastes sweet and feels hot, like she's ignited an inferno inside of me with just one kiss. She moves her mouth under mine, and I run my tongue along the seam of her lips until she opens to me and our tongues dance together.

Eventually, reluctantly, we part, but I lean my forehead on hers, not ready to fully lose this connection.

"Does that tell you what to do about it?" I whisper.

Summer nods, her eyes closed while mine roam her face, memorizing every inch.

"Can we do it again?"

"Absolutely."

And I do. I kiss her over and over until I'm fairly certain I'm drunk on her kisses. The world is spinning, and everything feels upside down and right side up at the same damn time.

This is what a kiss should be. How the fuck have I gone thirty-two years without experiencing this?

"You're really good at that," Summer says when we separate. Her lips are swollen and the delicate pink colour has spread, tinting her tanned skin. She licks her lips and looks around with a sheepish smile. "But I don't think we're in the best spot for a major make out session."

I chuckle. "Yeah, probably not." But the truth is, now that I've had a taste, there is no way I can resist her anymore.

Summer stands up and reaches her hand down to me. I take it, linking our fingers together and we continue to walk through the market.

"Ethan!" A familiar voice calls out my name and we turn to see someone waving. My face breaks into a wide grin when I realize who it is.

"Finn McNeil!" I cry and tug Summer gently in the direction of my old roommate from university. Finn and I greet each other with hugs and back slaps. He's standing out front of a vendor stall advertising a new winery.

"What's going on, man?" I ask.

Finn grins at me, glancing down to where my hand has joined with Summer's again. When he speaks, excitement bleeds into every word he says.

"Actually, I just moved here for a job. Pierre Monsat brought me on as master vintner for his new winery, La Lune Rouge. It's actually fairly close to your hometown. I was thinking of getting in touch with you for a beer and maybe a tour? I'm gonna need someplace to live."

"That sounds great," I say, and I mean it. Finn and I were roommates for most of our time in university, and we stayed in touch even after I moved back home to Dogwood Cove and he went down to California for a job.

"Finn, this is Summer. We grew up together in Dogwood Cove and she recently moved back."

Finn shakes Summer's free hand, his easy grin dancing between us. "Childhood sweethearts?"

Summer laughs. "Not exactly. His younger sister is my best friend and we, well," she looks over to me warmly. "We're exploring things."

I smile down at her, tugging her in closer to my side.

"Awesome. Well, let me give you guys a bottle of wine to try and Ethan, I'll give you a call tomorrow to set up some time to hang out soon." Finn reaches over to the table behind him and quickly perusing the bottles lined up, chooses one and passes it to Summer. "This is our latest Merlot. It's robust but soft on the palate, with hints of blackberry and plum. Perfect with a nice, seared filet mignon, if you can convince this guy to cook for you." Finn winks as I raise my eyebrows at his teasing.

"Thank you," Summer says, leaning over to give Finn a quick hug. "It was really great to meet you."

"You, too. Keep this guy in line, eh?" He nods over at me before shaking my hand heartily. He waves us off, then turns to some more customers and we walk away, Finn's booming laugh following us.

"Damn, Finn McNeil in town. That'll make things interesting," I say with a laugh of my own. Summer takes my hand again.

"He seems really nice."

"He is. Man, the shit we got up to in college," I shake my head, chuckling at the memories.

We continue walking, perusing the vendors, content to hold hands and enjoy each other. When Summer stops to admire some bouquets of flowers, I buy one for her just to see her face light up with happiness when I give it to her.

Eventually, we finish at the market and slowly make our way back to my truck.

"I don't want today to end," Summer says wistfully as I open her door. I spin her around, so her back is against the side of my truck and bring my hands up to frame her head. Slowly I lean forward, watching her eyes flutter closed, then I kiss her, brushing my lips across hers softly.

"If today doesn't end, then tomorrow can't begin. And tomorrow could be even better than today."

"Mmm. Good point," she mumbles against my lips, her arms winding around my neck. When she pulls me in for a deeper kiss, I go, willingly. This woman can have me anyway, anywhere, anytime she wants. Her kisses are a drug I can't get enough of and losing myself to them is the greatest high.

We drive home with her in the middle, leaning against me the same as she did earlier. But instead of my arm being stretched out behind her, it's trapped in her lap, her fingers covering mine, tracing small circles on my skin. We could be living in a country music song right now; this moment is so idyllic.

The sun is setting behind us as we turn off the highway and make our way down the road toward the bakery and Summer's apartment. I pull up out front and kill the engine but make no move to get out. It feels like the magic spell that has surrounded us all afternoon might break the second I leave this truck.

"What was that about tomorrow?" comes Summer's quiet teasing.

"I'm going to see you again tomorrow, right?" I say in a low voice.

"I certainly hope so."

"And I'll get to kiss you again?" I have to ask. I have to know that what has blossomed between us today isn't going to disappear now that we're home, around our friends and family.

I hear her intake of breath before Summer turns to me and pulls my face toward her with one hand. She presses a sweet but firm kiss to my lips, and when she pulls back, there's fire in her eyes.

"I certainly hope so. In fact, if you *don't* kiss me again tomorrow, Ethan Monroe, you'll be in trouble."

"What about Mila?" I wince, but I know we have to discuss my sister at some point. "She might be weird about this."

"We'll talk to her about it. About us." Summer's voice falters. "But maybe not right away? We can keep this between us for now, right?"

Part of me wants to protest, but who knows how Mila will react to me dating her best friend. Maybe it's better Summer and I figure things out between us first.

"So, there is an us?"

Goddamnit, why am I the vulnerable one today?

"Yes, Ethan. There is most definitely an us."

"Thank fuck." I huff out a breath I didn't know I was holding and finally climb down from the truck, jog around to open her door, and walk her up to her apartment.

When we get to the top of the stairs, I can't help but kiss her again. "I'll see you tomorrow, shorty."

Then, before I give in to temptation, I jog down the stairs and climb into my truck. I drive home on autopilot, my mind firmly focused on Summer. Kissing her felt like coming home. Like she was the answer to a prayer I didn't know I had.

And a little bit like jumping off a cliff, not knowing how deep the water runs.

Chapter 9

Summer

How do you sleep after what was arguably one of the best days of your life? Quite well, if you're me. When my alarm goes off early the next morning, I wake up with a smile and absolutely no inclination to hit the snooze button. Everything seems brighter, more hopeful today. I half expect birds to start singing and forest animals to talk to me, I'm so happy. *Mmm, Ethan dressed as Prince Charming. Yes, please.* With a giggle I roll over and stuff my face into my pillow. I've never been this excited over a man.

After a moment of indulging my girly freak out, I get up and pull on some shorts and a hoodie. The weather promises to be warm for June, and I'm excited to get some work done out at the cabins. I still haven't figured out how I'll pay for everything that's needed, but for now I'm just doing what I can.

I skip down the stairs and push open the door to the bakery.

"Mila? I smell muffins!" I call out, taking an appreciative sniff of the warm aroma of cinnamon and spice.

"In the kitchen," she hollers back. I pour a coffee and go to the back to find her cutting out scones from a round pile of dough.

"Hey girl, how was the market?"

Her question makes me freeze, my mug halfway to my mouth. I didn't realize she knew we were going to the market, which makes me wonder, what else does she know?

"It was fun. We ran into one of Ethan's old friends from college," I say casually, taking a sip of my coffee.

"Cool," she says distractedly, staying focused on her task. "Oh, Ethan said he was dropping by this morning. I thought the three of us could talk about the work party." Mila hands me a plate of warm muffins. "Take these out front for us to eat and I'll be there as soon as I take the next batch out."

I nod and take the plate, ducking my head to try and hide my blush. Either she doesn't know anything, or she's really good at hiding her reaction. No matter what, I'm not saying a word until I've talked to Ethan about how best to handle this.

"Okay, yeah, sounds good." I turn and hurry out of the kitchen, mentally preparing myself to see Ethan and *not* climb him like a tree in front of Mila.

As soon as I put the plate down on one of the bistro tables, the front door opens and in he walks. My breath catches at the sight of him. I have a newfound appreciation for ball caps and plaid, thanks to this man. When he sees me, a joyful grin stretches across his handsome face and I'm pretty sure my heart melts into a puddle of goo inside my chest. He walks over and before I can warn him that Mila could come out at any second, he's grabbing my face in his large hands, cradling it gently. The second his lips touch mine; we ignite. I slant my mouth over his mouth, my tongue seeking his tongue, my lips crushing his lips.

The sound of Mila working in the kitchen makes me pull back, and I see my guilt mirrored in Ethan's face.

"Sorry," I whisper.

He smiles quickly, his fingers ghosting across my cheek. "It's not your fault that I can't seem to resist kissing you."

I can feel the blush creeping across my face again; damn, he's swoony. But I make myself take a step back just in time as Mila comes out with a notebook and pen. I raise my eyebrows at that, but Ethan only chuckles and goes to sit down, taking a giant bite of a muffin before speaking.

"Alright, sister of mine, wow us with your organizational prowess. Let's plan a work party."

When Mila has to open the bakery for the day, we go our separate ways. Ethan said he was on his way to his office, promising to come and help me at Oceanside in the afternoon. After a quick stop at the hardware store for a new set of heavy-duty work gloves, I climb into my old truck and drive to the resort. Coming down the drive and seeing the mess I still have in front of me doesn't freak me out that much today. Sure, I still need to come up with thousands of dollars to pay for all the supplies and labor I'm sure to need for renovations, not to mention there's bound to be lots of costs associated with outfitting the cabins and getting everything functional again. But somehow, today I'm filled with optimism. I am well aware that kissing Ethan this morning is at least partially responsible for my good mood. The man's got magic lips, I swear. But fast on the heels of that thought comes worry. I can't lie to Mila or the other girls for long. That's just not who I am.

But I shake off those misgivings for now. The sun is shining and I'm ready to work. So, I crank some music through the speaker of my phone and get to it, hauling more junk to the growing pile that has to go to the dump.

The upbeat sounds of my eighties music playlist is interrupted mid-chorus of one of my favourite songs with the alert of a new text message. Glancing at my phone, I grin. The chat between us four girls is going on strong with conversation about book club and the lack of eligible men in town. Serena is particularly vocal about this problem.

SERENA: Let me just say, if Ethan doesn't make it his mission to recruit single young men to the town, he's dead to me.

MILA: Pretty sure he has other things to worry about. You know, like parking permits.

PAIGE: That is very derogative toward your brother's job, Mila.

MILA: Come on. He's mayor of a town of less than ten thousand people. How hard could it be.

PAIGE: As a matter of fact, the true ordinance of Mayor for a town such as Dogwood Cove is quite fascinating.

SERENA: OMG Paige. Go back to talking about romance novels, please!!!

PAIGE: Fine. Although may I add that your observation about the dearth of single men in town is a valid concern. Towns die out when the population growth slows down. A trend that is inevitable when your female population of breeding age outnumbers your virile male population.

MILA: Calling us breeding age feels wrong somehow.

SERENA: Agreed.

PAIGE: Perhaps your aversion to admitting that you are of the age to procreate can be a future discussion point for book club? There are plenty of surprise baby/accidental pregnancy romances we can read.

SERENA: Anything to do with accidental pregnancy might make me have a panic attack, Paige.

MILA: Same. No babies.

I chuckle under my breath as I wander over to the chair that I arranged to face the water and sit down. I'm not used to having girlfriends to gossip with, so this whole thing seems a little foreign but in a really good way. Although I haven't contributed anything to the conversation today, it's been a lot of fun being a part of the banter, even from the sidelines. Even so, after a few minutes break, I know I need to get back to work.

It would be way too easy to waste the day watching the waves and texting with my new friends.

SUMMER: Okay ladies, as entertained as I am reading this riveting chat, I need to get back to my tunes and my work. You interrupted Journey mid chorus. I need to know if I should stop believing.

MILA: Don't stop. Hold onto that feeling.

SERENA: Ooooh I should plan a recital using all 80's songs.

MILA: OMG yes. So cute.

PAIGE: I appreciate the music of the 80's but the hairstyles were abysmal. Please don't recreate those in your recital.

SUMMER: LOL. Definitely not.

Laughing to myself, I turn my music back on and the volume up high. Back to work.

A couple of hours later, I'm sweaty and tired. I lost the hoodie an hour ago, leaving me in a tank top and my shorts. My hair is sticking out of my pony tail every which way, and I'm pretty sure I have dirt smudged across both cheeks. But the interior of the main resort building is officially emptied and sort of cleaned. My hips are still bouncing and swaying to the music blaring out of my phone when I hear a familiar chuckle as warm hands slide over my hips.

"I see your dance moves haven't improved much over the years."

"What are you talking about? These hips don't lie," I say, giving an extra wiggle. Ethan's grip clenches into my side, and his lips brush my bare shoulders.

"Mmm. Salty and sweet." He mumbles against my skin. I twist around, bringing us face to face, and reach around to cup his ass. I give it a good squeeze, earning a raised eyebrow and a smirk from Ethan.

"Did you come here to work, or to distract me?"

"Can't I do both?"

Ethan bends down and picks me up, bringing my legs around his waist. I shriek with surprise as he turns and strides out of the building and takes me to the bed of his truck where the tailgate is conveniently lowered. He sets me down gently, his hands trailing around my ass and down my thighs to where my shorts end and he meets my skin. Goosebumps follow wherever he touches, and I shiver as his lips draw a line along my jaw and down my neck. I tilt my head to the side, letting my eyes drift closed. He slowly pulls one strap of my tank top down, taking my bra strap down with it and leaving it hanging off my shoulder. His lips follow, kissing and licking over my collarbone. He nips, I gasp. He sucks, I moan. I was sweaty before, but now I feel my internal temperature rising with every touch. There's a fire inside of me, and he's stoking it higher and higher. When he cups my breasts, the heat from his touch singes me even over the fabric of my clothing.

"Fucking hell, Summer, you're addicting," he groans, coming up to kiss me deeply, his lips crushing mine.

An impossible level of need fills me; the need to see him and touch him the way he's touching me. But when I reach for the bottom of his shirt, his hands come up to cover mine, stopping me.

"Why?" I ask, hearing a very plaintive sound in my own voice.

"Because" Ethan says, and his voice is rough like gravel. "You deserve better than some fooling around in the back of my truck."

He drops his forehead to mine and brings his palms down to the tailgate on either side of me. I bring my hands up to touch his chest and slide them up and over his shoulders.

"If it's up to me, I'm totally okay with fooling around in the back of your truck," I tease gently, earning a chuckle.

"I know you are. But I want to do this right, Summer." His eyes lift to meet mine, and I see something in them that makes me pause. Something that hits deeper than the out of control lust that's been coursing between us these last few moments.

"So far, you're doing just fine."

"Damnit woman, I want to take you on a real date first, so stop being so tempting," he growls, then slams his lips back onto mine, taking me by surprise. His hands go to my lower back, and he pulls me forward until my core is lined up with his very hard dick. My panties flood with damp heat, and when my legs lock around his waist again, holding him against me, I can't stop my hips from swiveling and grinding against him.

"Fuck," he curses again as he breaks away, taking a step back. His shoulders are heaving and he's staring at me with such intensity. Then he turns and walks away a short distance, running his fingers through his hair. I'm frozen on the tailgate, uncertain if I should go to him or stay here. Embarrassment starts to fill me as I realize I was basically dry humping him after he told me he didn't want to fool around in the back of his truck. I hop down and start to go back to the building to finish my work when Ethan grabs my hand.

"Summer, wait," he says, and the fire that was present before has been replaced with something else. Regret? Disgust? I don't know.

"Hey, what's with the tears?" His thumbs come up and brush away tears I didn't even know were spilling from my eyes. "Aww, Summer, babe, I didn't mean to hurt you. Shit. Come here."

Ethan pulls me into his arms and like a sick puppy dog desperate for attention, I go.

"Summer. I want you. I want you so fucking bad, my dick is literally hating me right now. But I also want to treat you right, which means taking you on a proper date, romancing you, hell, wooing you if need be, before I get you in bed."

I don't respond right away, letting his words sink in and heal the part of my heart that is programmed to expect rejection and abandonment. Eventually, I look up and the worried smile he's giving me proves that he means what he's saying. I lick my lips, and his gaze darkens before he bends down slowly, giving me time to turn away. I don't, and when his mouth meets mine, I drink in his affection, feeling his desire fill me.

This time, I'm the one who pulls back first.

"Okay. So, woo me."

Chapter 10

Ethan

After Summer threw down her challenge to me, we managed to put aside our hormones and focus on the cleanup around the resort. She put me to work loading up both of our trucks with all kinds of trash and junk, which we then carted away to the dump before going back for another load. It was sweaty, smelly, backbreaking work, and exactly what I needed to keep my hands off her.

It took a couple of hours, but eventually the piles of garbage were gone. I have to admit that in a very short period of time, Summer has done a lot around here. The resort is looking a lot better, and it's all thanks to her effort. But there's no denying that the list of things still to be done is huge. I want to help, and I will, whether in labor, tools, supplies, or support. Anything I can do to help her make this happen, I will do.

When the last load is dumped, we head back to the resort to pick up some things we left behind. Summer is still so beautiful, even with her hair a mess and dirt smeared across her clothes. The bandage on her leg reminds me of the other day when she cut herself, and the soft expression on her face when I kissed her leg right above the cut. Her surprise quickly turned to heat, and that was when I knew she was in this as much as I was.

"Good God, what I wouldn't give for a hot bath."

My dick stirs at her words, and when I glance up from where I'm putting my tools back in my truck, I see Summer arching her back. She may only be stretching, but the position pushes her tits forward in a way that is all too inviting.

"Christ, do you even know how fucking sexy you are?" I grind out the words, shamelessly adjusting myself with a smirk when I see her watching. "If you want someone to volunteer to wash your back, I'm your guy. After I take you on our date."

She sashays over to me, and I know she's throwing an extra sway in her step just to mess with me. "You keep teasing me by talking about all the things you'll do to me, then throwing down the 'after our date' part. If you're trying to make me even hornier by making me wait, it won't work."

I cock an eyebrow. "And why's that?"

She leans in close enough to whisper, her breath hot against my ear. "Because my panties are already soaked, and my body is already vibrating. Pretty sure I can't get any more desperate for you than this."

I let out a growling noise as I cover her lips with mine, sucking hard, nipping at her lower lip until she lets me in. Our bodies clash together, sweat and dirt mingling between us. All the pent-up passion from the afternoon is let loose in our kiss and it's the rawest, most erotic kiss of my life. She moans into my mouth when my hands get caught in her hair, and it doesn't take an idiot to realize she enjoyed the sensation of her hair being pulled. But still I experiment, tugging gently as my lips travel to her ear.

"You like that?" I whisper hoarsely, and she lets out a moan of agreement. Her hands move to the bottom of my shirt, and unlike earlier, this time I let her lift it up and over my head, silently vowing to myself it won't go further than this. But fuck, do I ever want to have her touching my body. Her eyes widen as she roams her gaze over my torso, and I've never been happier to have been blessed with the body I have. Don't get me wrong; regular runs, plus having outdoor activities at my fingertips from living on the west coast have helped, but good ol' genetics gave me the predisposition for the six-pack she's currently running her fingers over.

"Fucking hell, Summer," I groan as her fingers skate around to my back. She splays her hand wide and pulls me forward, until our chests are pressed together. I want so badly to strip her shirt off and feel her skin on mine, but I won't. Not yet. Not even if it kills me to hold back.

She steps back first, and I'm glad she's strong enough to do so. Lord knows I'm not.

"This date needs to happen soon, Ethan," she pants. Her chest is heaving and my eyes zero in on her tits without a care. Until she pokes me in my still naked chest. "I'm up here buddy, and put a shirt on, would you? Those muscles are distracting."

I huff out a frustrated laugh at that. "You're the one who took if off of me," I say, bending down and picking my shirt up.

"I know. Sorry. I was caught up in the moment until I remembered your crazy rule about going on a date before giving me my first man-made orgasm in over a year."

Oh, hell no. She did *not* just say that.

I toss my shirt to the ground behind me without a care and take the two steps that separate us in one long stride. Leaning down I grab her around her luscious ass and lift her up in my arms.

"Woah there, lumberjack, where are you going?" she cries as I hurry over to the large, flat rock that overlooks the ocean and we've been using as a seat.

I sit down with her on my lap and pull her face forward and kiss her firmly.

"This is gonna be fast and messy, and nowhere near enough for what you deserve, but my girl needs to be taken care of."

"Wait, what?" Summer says, but my intention becomes clear when I lean back, reach between us and unbutton her shorts. My fingers slide deftly inside, stroking the outside of her panties. She wasn't lying, they're drenched.

"Oh my God, Ethan," she gasps when I reach beneath her panties and part her folds. She leans down and kisses me as her body starts to undulate around my fingers. Her hands are clenched in my hair, holding me to her. I slick my fingers back and forth, teasing her, but not for long.

I need to feel her tighten around me. I need to feel her explode around me.

When I insert one, then two fingers into her, Summer cries out and arches into me, holding onto my shoulders and throwing her head back. I lean down and press kisses up her throat and along her jaw, as her body rocks to a rhythm only she can hear.

When I press my thumb on her clit, and curl my fingers slightly, her hands tighten their grip on my shoulders.

"Yes, oh God, please, yes more, more, more, more, oh God, Ethan, *Ethan!*" She comes apart in a spectacular release, her muscles clenching around my fingers like a vise, her hands grasping at me desperately. Her body is shuddering as I kiss her anywhere that I can reach, still slowly sliding my fingers in and out to draw out her climax. Eventually I pull my hand free when her movements still, and her head drops down on my shoulder. I look down at her to make sure she's watching as I lift my fingers to my mouth and lick them one by one.

"You're fucking delicious, Summer." The words come out hoarse, and the arousal in her eyes isn't dimmed in the slightest. My cock is throbbing, aching to be set free, but the satisfied hum coming from her is all I need right now.

"I'm taking you on that date tomorrow night."

By the time I get home from the resort, my body is aching, and not only from the hard work I put in there. Heading straight to my en suite, peeling off dirty clothes as I go, I turn my shower on as hot as I can stand it and step under the spray. After letting the hot water pound down on me for a minute to try and ease some of my tired muscles, I quickly soap up and finish my shower. Once I'm done, I step out, dry off, and pull on a pair of old sweats before walking into the kitchen to deal with my growling stomach. Thank God for leftovers is all I can say, because I sure as shit don't have the brain power to cook right now. I shovel cold spaghetti into my mouth and grab a glass of water. Taking my dinner, I go straight to the couch and turn on the TV. Even if the Canucks didn't make the Stanley Cup playoffs this year, I'm still a good ol' Canadian boy who needs his hockey fix.

UNKNOWN: Hey, it's Summer. Mila gave me your number... So we can talk about renovations *winky face emoji*

When the message pops up on my phone, I grin. I can't believe I forgot to get Summer's phone number, but then again we were a little distracted. Looks like she took care of things herself. I turn the TV on mute and settle into the couch before typing out my reply.

ETHAN: Gotta say, Shorty, I admire your crafty-ness.

SUMMER: How else would I be able to thank you for today?

SUMMER: And I'm not talking about renovations.

ETHAN: Damn, woman.

SUMMER: I'm excited for tomorrow.
ETHAN: Me too.

We go back and forth a while longer over text, and even though part of me wants to take it a step further and call her, I don't. I'm banking on anticipation making tomorrow night all the more spectacular.

Everything is set up for this evening when I get up the next morning. I put fresh sheets on the bed, and make sure there is a bottle of wine chilling in the fridge. I'm not going to automatically assume we'll end up back here after what I have planned, but I sure as fuck hope we do.

The anticipation for tonight is running through my body like a low-level electrical current and I know I need to chill out if I'm going to get anything done today. So, I lace up and head out into the cool spring morning for a run. The grass is dewy, but flowers are starting to bloom. Honestly, springtime on Vancouver Island is fucking gorgeous. It's lush and green, and if you can handle the frequent rain, there's a lot of beauty around here. As my feet pound the pavement, I let my mind drift to other things I want to do with Summer. Hikes to some local waterfalls, hot springs, daytrips to the mainland or over to some of the smaller islands.

I stop to catch my breath and stretch once my lungs are sufficiently burning. My phone ringing is just the excuse I need to call it quits; it's almost time to shower and go to the office anyway. I turn and start walking home as I answer the call with a grin.

"Hey, Finn."

"Ethan! How's it goin' man? Listen, I'm coming to town next week, was hoping I could take you up on the offer to show me around? I need to get out of this hotel and find a place to live soon." Finn's voice booms into my ear. He's still larger than life with his energy and personality.

"Yeah, that sounds great. What day are you thinking?"

"Let's say, next Thursday?"

"Perfect. Tell me more about this winery."

Finn lets out a hoot of excitement. "Oh fuck, man it's incredible. Pierre has apparently been following my work down in California, and when he heard I was looking for a new challenge he was over the top excited. Couldn't offer me the partnership fast enough. I was more than ready to head back north of the border, so here I am. He found a property about twenty minutes outside of Dogwood Cove, there's a little bit of land if we want to try growing our own grapes, but the plan is mostly to import from the Okanagan and just make our own vintages from it. Right now, it's a blank void of a building, but there's space for a tasting room, maybe even a bistro. It's gonna be amazing."

"That's incredible." I'm truly happy for my friend. We've stayed in touch ever since graduating, and I've watched him make quite the name for himself at a winery in Napa, winning all kinds of awards as the lead vintner.

Finn and I chat a while longer until I get home. With our plans for next week confirmed, I quickly shower and dress for a workday at city hall, forcing my attention to what I need to accomplish there in the next eight hours.

That's all that stands between me and getting Summer in my arms, and hopefully in my bed tonight.

Chapter 11

Summer

It's a really good thing I'm not trying to use power tools or anything of the sort today. All I can think about are Ethan's hands bringing me to ecstasy yesterday, and how much further things could go tonight. He won't tell me what he has planned, only to *dress sexy*. When I got that text message, my whole body shivered with anticipation. Sweet and caring Ethan clearly has a dirty side, and I am having way too much fun uncovering that.

My head is still in the clouds when I walk into Harbour Dance, Serena's studio, in the late afternoon. She's teaching a toddler tap class, and I watch through the large glass window as she leads the most adorable group of kids around the room with her arms floating up and down. The click clack of tap shoes can be heard over the quiet voices of the parents watching the class, some of whom glance at me curiously. I don't recognize any of them, but that's not exactly a surprise given how long I was gone from Dogwood Cove.

Several minutes later, Serena wraps up class with a clap of her hands, and the hyper group of kids come rushing into the waiting area with their noisy shoes creating a cacophony of sound. Serena waves me through, and I weave through kids and moms until I am in the main studio.

"Hey, Summer! Thanks for coming by," she says breezily as she goes over to the sound system.

Serena's got an ethereal elegance to her; she glides instead of walks. Her dance background is apparent in every move she makes. I feel frumpy and awkward in comparison, but brush off the critical thought like a fly buzzing in my ear. I don't waste time on feeling bad about myself for long. That was not an option after watching my mother overcompensate for her low self-esteem in man after man, none of whom stuck around long.

"Hi, thanks again for agreeing to let me teach a few classes here," I say, pulling out my yoga mat. Serena wanted me to run her through several different styles of classes so we can decide what to offer. "I've got a fit and flow practice, a slower paced hatha, and I was thinking we could offer an evening unwind class as well."

She waves her hand at me. "Honestly, you're doing me a favour. I didn't want to figure out adult classes, so you've solved my problem for me. Those three options all sound perfect."

I smile, gratified that I'm not just being given a handout with the opportunity to teach here.

Serena grabs her mat and we get started. I run her through shortened versions of the classes I am proposing, and we go through the practices with ease. It's not surprising to me that Serena has the flexibility and strength to get into some of the more challenging postures, but when she collapses out of a forearm stand at the end, we both fall onto our mats giggling.

"Oh man. Okay, yep, let's offer those classes to start, and I'll be coming to the fit and flow class!" Serena puffs out some air, making the hair that has fallen over her face fly up in the air.

I sit up and wrap my arms around my knees. "Really? So, all three classes?"

She sits and faces me. "Yeah, I think they will all be really popular. We might have to offer more than one session of them." Her face turns serious. "I know how much work you've got to do out at the resort, are you sure you can commit to this? I hate to sound like a nag, but I don't want to set all of this up, only to have you needing to cancel after a month or so."

I hurry to shake my head. "No way, that won't happen. I love teaching yoga, it grounds me. Yes, the resort will need a lot of my time, but I can definitely fit in these classes."

"Okay, then let's get these on the schedule and start signing people up." Serena claps her hands, much as she did at the end of the tap class, and unfolds her long body, standing up gracefully. We roll up our mats and after agreeing on a schedule and fee structure, I leave her to teach her next class.

When I get back to the apartment above the bakery, I head straight for the shower. As the hot water beats down on my hair, I close my eyes and let my imagination carry me forward to tonight. Despite the heat from the water, I shiver thinking about what I want to do with Ethan. What I want him to do *to me.*

After finishing my shower and drying my hair, I stand in front of my closet in my bra and panties, surveying my meager wardrobe. I have never been one to own too many clothes, and definitely not anything fancy. Ethan wants me to dress sexy, but I honestly don't think I have anything that fits that description. I have one pair of heels, and they're booties. Some jeans that make my ass look great, but wouldn't a skirt or a dress be sexier? I guess I don't have a choice there, since my only options are casual summer dresses. Hanging behind my favourite cozy sweater, I see a flash of red. Recognition dawns, that's the shirt I bought six months ago when I thought I was going on a date with a Henry Cavill look alike. The guy turned out to be a total dud, and looked *nothing* like superman, but at least I have that shirt.

When I'm dressed and have applied a little bit of makeup, I take one final look in the mirror. *Not bad.* The jeans really do make my ass look phenomenal, and the way the red blouse is cut in the front, it shows the perfect amount of cleavage. The secret weapon is the cut out in the back that dips almost down to my bra strap, but not quite. It's sexy but subtle. And I'm confident it'll be enough to drive Ethan wild, especially if I keep it covered with a coat at first.

I'm putting on a coat of light lip gloss when I hear his footsteps on the stairs leading up to the apartment. I grin at myself in the mirror, my body humming with excitement. Opening the door, my heart stops dead.

Ethan in a plaid shirt is one sexy lumberjack look-alike. Ethan in a snug, dark blue, button-down shirt and tailored dress pants is a walking, talking orgasm.

"Wow," he murmurs, his beautiful lips curving into a smile.

"That was my line," I say weakly as I reach out and grab his hand, pulling him into my apartment. I wrap my arms around his neck and lift up on my toes to kiss him, breathing in his scent, so clean, so manly, so...Ethan.

"Mmm, as much as I want to continue this, we gotta go." Ethan pulls back, keeping his hands on my hips.

I pout but reach over and grab my purse off the kitchen counter. "Fine. Let the wooing commence."

His rich chuckle fills my ears as we leave my apartment.

"When was the last time you were in Victoria?"

We're driving out of town toward the highway, and I'm staring hungrily at his profile, strong and solid. Ethan is all man, and simply being around him grounds me in a way nothing else does.

I have to think about his question for a minute. "Does driving past the exit for downtown on my way here count?"

He shakes his head with a small grin.

"Then it would have been that time your parents took us all in to go to the museum. Are we going to Victoria tonight?" He won't tell me anything about the date he's got planned, but my pulse quickens at the thought of a romantic dinner in the city with Ethan.

"Yes, and that's all I'm telling you." He winks at me. He knows that I'm going crazy not knowing the plan. "We'll have to come back one day during daylight. Hit up the waterfront, go to the museum, Butchart Gardens." His hand is resting casually over mine on my thigh, his thumb stroking across the back of my hand.

"I'd like that," I say, turning to face him. He flashes me a quick smile before turning his eyes back to the road. We're planning future dates and we haven't even finished our first one yet. That must be a good sign.

Twenty minutes later, we come to a stop behind a lineup of cars. Ethan's frowning, and turns on the radio to a local traffic station, just in time to hear the announcer talk about a multi-vehicle accident on the highway.

"Shit. There's no other easy way to the city," Ethan curses. "We might be late."

I touch his shoulder. "Seeing as I have no idea where we're going or what we're doing, that's fine with me."

He chuckles at that. "Good point. Maybe I shouldn't have said anything and you never would have known."

"Well," I say wryly, "The traffic jam probably isn't part of your plan, so I think I would have guessed something was wrong."

Half an hour later we are finally past the accident and moving at speed again. Ethan is tense, both hands gripping the steering wheel. I want to reassure him that I don't mind if we're late or if plans have to change, I just want to be with him. But he seems so stressed, glancing at the clock every thirty seconds, I say nothing.

Traffic in the city is also unusually heavy, the added delays making Ethan more frustrated. When we pull up to the harbour, right before eight o'clock, he sags in his seat before turning his head to look at me.

"We had a seven thirty reservation at Savour," he says, naming a fancy restaurant overlooking the water. "I doubt they'll honor it with us being so late, but we can try."

I slide across the bench seat until I'm pressed up against him. Holding his face between my hands, I press two quick kisses to his lips. Firm enough that he knows I'm not messing around, but quick enough not to get sidetracked by how damn good of a kisser he is.

"I don't care if we eat at the fanciest restaurant in the city or a park bench. I'm out with you, this is our first date, and after this we're going to have hot sex," I say. "That's all that matters."

That gets a laugh out of him at last, and he leans over to kiss me deeply. I let him take his time, his tongue coming out to explore my mouth, and his hands going to my low back.

"I just wanted everything to be perfect for you tonight," he whispers against my skin. His eyes are closed, but mine are open, drinking in his long eyelashes, the freckle underneath his right eye, and his rugged cheekbones. When my fingertips tickle the skin on the side of his neck, he opens his eyes, and the disappointment there kills me.

"Do you honestly think I'm going to be upset about missing a fancy dinner reservation? Ethan, it's me. Let's go get a slice of pizza and park the truck someplace pretty where we can make out."

"You sure?" There's a vulnerable edge to his voice.

"Yes. Totally sure."

Ethan flashes me a much more confident smile. "Okay then, I know a place." He puts the truck in drive and pulls out. A few moments later, he parks once more, this time in front of a tiny pizzeria with a neon sign out front that says *Gino's*.

"Wait here," he says to me. As he's about to close the truck door, he pulls it open again. "Anything you hate on pizza?"

"Olives," I say with a smile. He nods, then shuts the door and walks inside. I watch, bemused, as he greets the man behind the counter with a handshake and one of those manly back slapping hugs. He walks back out and climbs into his seat.

"One hot pie coming in ten minutes."

"Who's that?" I ask, curious about this new layer of Ethan I'm uncovering. He knows a guy who owns a pizza joint in Victoria. I did *not* see that coming.

"Gino? He owns the place. Dad and I used to go camping down in Gold Creek each year. We'd always stop in for a pie on the way to the campground," Ethan says with a smile, leaning his head back against the seat. "I still make sure to come by every time I'm in town. Best pizza on Vancouver Island."

Half an hour later, the pizza is gone, and I'm wishing I wasn't wearing skinny jeans. We found a bench in a nearby park, and devoured the hot, cheesy pie. I don't want to hurt Ethan's feelings, but I honestly think this was better than dinner at Savour.

"Well, I guess I can cross eating the best pizza on Vancouver Island off of my bucket list," I say, leaning back with a groan. Ethan laughs and stretches his legs out in front of him, his thigh pressed against mine. His arm lifts behind my shoulder, and I snuggle into his side.

"I'll never steer you wrong when it comes to pizza. Next time we'll try his barbecue chicken pie. It's incredible."

There he goes making future date plans again. Swoony bastard. A cold wind whips through and I shiver involuntarily. This outfit might look cute, but the jacket is not a warm one.

"Come on, shorty. Time to go home before you turn into an icicle."

This time I shiver from something other than the cold.

But when we get home to Dogwood Cove, Ethan doesn't drive to his house. He pulls up in front of the bakery and puts the truck in park before turning to me.

"First, believe me that this physically pains me to admit," he begins with a wry grin. "But it's safe to say tonight didn't go as planned."

"I had a great time," I interject, hearing the needy tone to my voice. Ethan must hear it, too, because he coughs back a groan before he continues.

"I did, too, Summer. But I meant it when I said I want to romance you. You deserve to be treated like a queen and I plan on doing just that. I care too much about you for this to just be about getting you in bed." He runs his hand through his hair, messing it up, and a petulant voice in my head says *I wanted to do that.* "I can't believe I'm saying this. But I'm not going upstairs with you. If I do, I won't want to leave. And we're not having sex tonight because you need a do-over date."

The romantic side of me is swooning; the horny side of me is cursing. Apparently, the only action I'm seeing tonight is going to be between me and my vibrator. Damn this man and his romantic morals.

"Fine. But this do-over date needs to happen really soon." I say with an over-the-top pout.

"Is tomorrow soon enough?"

Chapter 12

Ethan

The universe really does *not* want me to get laid. First it was the goddamn traffic jam and missing our reservations in Victoria, although Summer's right — pizza in the park ended up being a lot of fun.

But now, I should be at home preparing dinner for Summer and lighting candles for a romantic atmosphere. Instead, I'm driving two hours north to my Great Aunt Marilyn's house because she called this morning to say her basement was full of water.

I texted Summer as I was loading up my truck with tools and supplies, but she hasn't replied yet and I left half an hour ago. Marilyn lives way the fuck out in the middle of nowhere, and I know the nearest store is a Walmart an hour away, so it's better to be prepared with anything I might need. I wish I had the chance to talk to Summer before leaving, but I needed to get on the road. My aunt isn't one to ask for help unless the situation is really bad. She's lived alone my entire life, and my mom always said she liked it that way.

All I can do now is hope that whatever I need to deal with doesn't take too long because my dick is already angry at me for passing up the chance to be with Summer last night. If I have to wait several more days to be with her, I might explode.

My phone finally rings when I'm close to my aunt's house.

"Hey pretty girl."

"Hi, I got your message. Have you already left town?" Disappointment colours her tone, and I hate that I'm the cause of it.

"Yeah, I got on the road pretty quick. I'm sorry, Summer. Marilyn doesn't have anyone else to call and it sounds bad. She's got almost an inch of water in her basement."

"Oh no, that's awful."

"It is, but missing my plans with you is worse," I say. And I'm not exaggerating. I feel bad for my aunt, and of course I want to help her, but fuck, am I upset about not being with Summer tonight.

"We'll have another chance. I'm not going anywhere," is her soft reply and it makes me smile.

"Damn right we will. When I get back, I'm not letting you out of my sight or out of my arms for several days," I growl, my hands tightening on my steering wheel.

"Promises, promises," she teases, and the sultry tone of her voice makes me crazy.

"Alright, I better go, I'm pulling up at Aunt Marilyn's house. Can I call you later?" I say, my voice tinged with regret.

"You better."

I end the call and sit for a moment in my truck. She's way too fucking good for me. What other woman would be that understanding of not one, but two failed dates?

I catch sight of Aunt Marilyn opening her front door and waving at me, so I climb down from my truck.

"Oh, hi honey, thank you so much for coming out right away," Marilyn sounds tired, but relieved, and instantly I know that no matter what happens with Summer, I made the right call. Family comes first.

"Hey, Aunt Marilyn, it's no trouble. Let's take a look at what's going on."

The moment I step into the basement, I realize I won't be back in Dogwood Cove by tomorrow like I had hoped. Even if I find the source of the leak and repair that, the cleanup down here is going to take a long time. Marilyn's got boxes everywhere, many of which show evidence of water damage on the bottom.

"I tried to move some boxes away from the water, but a few things got wet," she frets, twisting her small hands together.

"I see that. Let's start with getting stuff out of here so I've got some space. Is there somewhere upstairs we can take them?"

Aunt Marilyn nods, and walks slowly up the stairs out of the basement to show me a space she's cleared in the corner of her kitchen.

"Alright, I'll get to work. Don't suppose you could make a pot of coffee?" I ask, knowing I've got a long day ahead. Marilyn's eyes light up, and I suspect she is happy to have something to do to help me.

"Absolutely, dear. Coming right up."

Several hours later the basement is emptied of boxes and Marilyn is busy sorting the contents into piles of items that can be salvaged, washed and kept, or need to be tossed. I've already told her I'll do a run to the dump later.

Thankfully, emptying the basement is a mindless task that gives me plenty of time to think of other things, namely, how to make it up to Summer. I briefly debate planning an overnight trip somewhere, but when you consider I haven't even taken her to bed, that seems presumptuous. Finally, I settle on the plan I had all along. A romantic, candlelit dinner at my house, and after, I can take her upstairs and worship her body the way she deserves.

I step outside for a break after carrying the last of the boxes upstairs and check my phone. Summer has been sending me photos of what she's working on at the resort. The most recent picture is a selfie of her, set against the ocean. She's so beautiful, it kills me that I'm not there right now.

ETHAN: Hey, how's the cleanup going at the resort?

SUMMER: Great. Your friends came back.

I chuckle at the picture she sends me of two raccoons glaring out the door of one of the cabins. She's never going to let me live that down. It's not my fault I think they're disgusting and infested with disease.

ETHAN: DAMNIT I said never to mention that again! And be careful. Please. Maybe skip that cabin?

SUMMER: Don't be a baby. I opened the door and they walked out. Easy peasy.

ETHAN: You take pleasure in mocking me.

SUMMER: I do.

ETHAN: I'll have to punish you for that later.

I see the bubble with three dots appear and disappear several times and wonder if that was too far. I start to type out an apology, when her response shows.

SUMMER: I might like that.

I groan, and crouch down in the dirt, letting my head fall forward. She's gonna be the death of me.

ETHAN: Fucking hell, Summer. It's killing me that I won't be with you tonight. The things I want to do to you...

SUMMER: Maybe you could call me tonight and tell me about them?

ETHAN: You're damn right I could. And I will.

SUMMER: You know what they say about absence making the heart grow fonder? Maybe anticipation makes something else... grow.

SUMMER: And on that cheesy innuendo, I've got to go and teach a yoga class. Talk to you tonight, lumberjack.

ETHAN: Can't wait.

I exhale loudly. Good thing Aunt Marilyn takes her hearing aids out to go to sleep at night.

"Hey lumberjack, what are you wearing?"

This is how Summer answers her phone tonight and I'm instantly hard the second I hear her voice.

"Nothing but plaid, baby," I tease.

"Seriously? That's hot." She giggles and I quickly snap a pic and send it to her.

"Oh, come on. Plaid jammies? Geez, Ethan, you don't play fair," she complains but I hear the laughter in her voice.

"Told you, all plaid." I drop my voice low for the last two words and Summer loses it, laughing hysterically.

"Hey, this was meant to be a sexy call."

"Sorry, sorry, I'll stop," she says in between chuckles. "Okay. I'm good. So, how was your day?"

"How was my day. That's what you want to talk about? Well, let's see. I spent it wading in an inch of cold, muddy water, cleaning up boxes of random shit that my aunt has been collecting. I got to drink weak-ass coffee because dear old Marilyn doesn't know how to make *real* coffee, and for dinner I got an overcooked pot roast instead of the salmon bake I was going to make for us."

"Poor baby. I wish I was there to make it better," she murmurs, and the whole tone of our conversation turns.

"Yeah? How would you do that?"

"Well, first, I'd repay the orgasm you gave me the other day at the resort." Her voice drops to a whisper. "I've thought about that a lot."

"Mmm. Me too," I rumble, reaching down to free my cock from my pants. "I've thought about how wet you were, how fuckin' good you tasted. I can't stop thinking about how you'll feel when I finally slide my dick inside."

Summer gasps, then lets out a little moan.

"Are you touching yourself?"

"Mmm hmm," she says, and my hand squeezes around my dick.

"Good. Imagine it's my hands sliding under your panties. Are you wet for me?"

"Yes," she says, and it comes out as a moan of a word. "Are you hard for me?"

"Fuck, Summer, if I was any harder, I could pound nails with my dick."

"God, Ethan. I wish I could feel you."

"You will, soon. I promise. I want your hands on me, and my mouth on you."

Her moans give me all the inspiration I need, and my hand quickens its motions, pulling up and down my cock. I would give anything for it to be her hand, or better yet her body, squeezing me right now. But maybe what she said earlier is right. Anticipation can only make things better.

"Ethan, I'm close," she cries out.

"I'm right there with you, shorty," I manage to ground out the words as a lightning fast orgasm comes barrelling toward me.

Summer's moans escalate, and I hear the catch in her voice when she cascades over the edge into her release and I follow with my own orgasm.

"Wow, that was fast," Summer says breathlessly.

"I can't help it, you're so goddamn sexy, I've turned into a two-pump chump," I chuckle wryly. "I promise to last longer when we're together for real."

"I'm not exactly complaining, now am I?"

My laugh comes out half groan, half rumble. "I do think I need a different nickname for you. Shorty isn't exactly the sexiest name, is it?"

"No, but I like it," she says quietly. "You're the only person who has ever called me that, and it's...I don't know...special. Our friendship feels like the foundation of this new relationship, and I don't want to ever lose sight of that."

I'm stunned into silence. I never realized it, but she's right.

"Shorty it is." I say, unable to think of anything better to respond with.

We're both silent for a moment, and I hope she's experiencing the same kind of intense connection that I am right now, despite us being many miles apart.

"I wish you were here, Ethan," she says in a whisper.

"God, so do I."

Before I go to sleep that night, on the very lumpy mattress in Aunt Marilyn's guest bedroom, I send a silent prayer to the renovation gods that the damage isn't too extensive, and I can get out of here quickly.

But the next morning, my prayer is proven to be in vain. Thanks to the fans and dehumidifiers I had running all night, the puddle that had previously covered the floor is mostly gone. But now, with the light of day and the basement empty of boxes, I can see exactly how bad the damage is. The drywall and insulation will all have to be ripped out and replaced, and I still haven't located the source of the leak. My suspicion is a broken water line somewhere in the ceiling between the basement and the main floor, but I won't know for sure until I rip down that ceiling. All of which means, I'm going to be here for longer than I originally thought.

Sighing inwardly, I open my phone to make some calls. First to my office, to let them know I won't be back until the end of the week. Then I text Mila to bring her up to date and finally, I make the call I really wish I didn't have to make.

"Hey, shorty, bad news," I say when Summer answers the phone.

"Oh no, is your aunt's house okay?"

"The water damage isn't quite as bad as I thought, but there's a lot of work to do. I'll get the drywall and ceiling taken down today, then I can deal with the leaking pipe. But there's more cleaning up to do, and I'll need to re-insulate and re-drywall before I can come home." I sigh. "Then I'll have to come back another time to finish off everything."

"I'll come with you next time and help," Summer says firmly.

"You're amazing, you know that?" I can't help but say.

"Me? No, you're the amazing nephew who dropped everything to go and help."

"You're more than that, Summer. You're the woman who understood me having to cancel plans last minute, who's patient and supportive, and offering to help." I pause, wanting her to really get how much that means to me. "I appreciate it, that's all."

"Well, feel free to express your appreciation to me in person when you get back," she says with a sassy tone that makes me grin.

"Trust me, I will."

Chapter 13

Summer

Today was yet another day of cleanup at the resort and trying to keep myself distracted from missing Ethan. Unfortunately, that meant I lost track of time and now I'm running late for book club. When I step out of the shower, there is a message waiting on my phone that makes me giggle.

ETHAN: Try not to have too much fun talking about imaginary men tonight, okay?

Wrapping a towel around myself I type out a reply.

SUMMER: Well since there's no real man around to entertain me...

ETHAN: Wow. I leave for three days and you move on without giving me a chance.

SUMMER: Book boyfriends do it better, or so I hear.

ETHAN: You heard wrong. And when I get home tomorrow, I'll prove it.

I flop down on my bed with a loud sigh, thankful that no one is around to see me blush. He certainly knows how to stir things up, even from a distance. I've had plenty of time this week to fantasize about being with Ethan, and something tells me reality will be even hotter than my wildest fantasy.

I just have to get through a night with the girls without letting anything slip about me and Ethan.

After some calming breaths I get up and finish getting dressed. We're meeting at Paige's house, a small cottage right off Main street. With two bottles of wine in hand, I lock up my apartment and set out on foot. No sense in driving when I'm pretty sure both bottles will be empty by the end of the evening.

When I get close to Paige's house, the front door flies open, and Mila hollers out at me.

"Get in here, Summer, I need a drink!"

Laughing, I pick up the pace and hurry up the path to Mila, who gestures impatiently for the bottles in my hands. I pass them over and step inside, taking off my jacket and shoes. Moving further into the house, I can hear Serena laughing, and the murmur of Paige's more subdued voice. I find them standing in the kitchen, where Mila is pouring generous glasses of wine. The kitchen island is covered in plates of different finger food and my mouth waters. Ethan's texts had me so distracted I forgot to eat dinner.

"Summer, we need you to be the voice of reason, please. Paige is trying to tell me that the story line is the most important aspect of the book. She obviously didn't read the shower scene. Right? I'm right, aren't I?" Serena is talking a mile a minute, and Paige is shaking her head.

"Umm, well, I mean, the story was good," I start lamely, not really wanting to take sides. Although, if I had to, Serena's right. That scene was hot.

"Focusing only on the intimate scenes discredits the talent of the writer who diligently worked to create intricate characters and plot," Paige argues, and I see her stabbing her finger down on a piece of paper in front of her. It looks a lot like the sheet of questions she gave me earlier in the week.

"It's a *romance* novel Paige, doesn't that imply that the romance is the most important part?" Serena executes an impressive eye roll, then pops a chip loaded with salsa into her mouth.

"Yes, the romance is a significant aspect, however, you must agree that the sex scenes were not integral to the plot. Really, the book was about Hazel's journey to overcome her fears of commitment, and open herself to love," Paige says primly, steepling her fingers on her paper.

"They've been arguing this for almost five minutes. I say we grab some snacks and go into the living room, see how long it takes them to notice we're gone," Mila whispers.

When we're each settled in one of the dark blue chairs that are set in front of the bay window, I take a long sip of wine. It's the first time I've been alone with Mila since Ethan and I started dating, if you can call it that, and I'm not really sure what to say. Even though it was my idea not to tell her about Ethan and I right away, I hate keeping the secret from her. I'm saved when Paige and Serena wander into the room, and I notice Serena is looking triumphant. Paige on the other hand, seems frustrated.

"Let's start the discussion, shall we?" Paige says, sitting down on the edge of the couch with her hands folded in her lap. "I trust you've all had a chance to review the discussion questions for tonight?"

Mila swings her legs over the arm of her chair, and tips her head back, striking the ultimate IDGAF pose. "Paige, honey, I love you, but relax. We read the book, we liked the book, we can talk about the book. But let's be honest. This is mostly a chance to get together and drink wine and eat lots of junk food once a month."

I hold back my laugh at the horrified expression on poor Paige's face. She's obviously the only one who takes the idea of a book club very seriously. Part of me wants to humor her and look at her questions, the other part agrees wholeheartedly with Mila. I just want to hang out with my friends for an evening.

"Let me see if I understand this correctly. I spent all this time crafting thought-provoking discussion questions, and all you want to do is drink wine and eat food?" Paige tilts her chin down, frowning at us like a schoolteacher scolding her wayward students.

"And talk about the sex scenes," Serena chimes in.

"Hear, hear," Mila raises her glass with a nod to Serena.

"Can we at least discuss one or two of my points?" Paige mutters.

"I enjoyed how Hazel was a confident badass," I offer, and Paige brightens, sitting up straighter.

"Yes! Thank you, Summer. I also found the character arc that Hazel underwent to be a very intriguing aspect. The way she —"

"The way he went to town eating her lady taco on the kitchen counter!" Serena interrupts, leaning over to nudge Paige with her shoulder.

If looks could kill, then the withering gaze Paige turns on Serena would be deadly. I hold back my giggle, sharing a glance with Mila, who rolls her eyes in response.

"Serena, you were just as enthusiastic about book club as I was. I don't understand why you won't at least try to consider the fact that the intimate encounters were not the only salient plot points worth discussing!"

"Because I haven't been laid in months and this book was basically porn with a little bit of plot."

Even I can't help but laugh at that.

Paige groans, and crumples up the paper in front of her. "Fine, I give up. Talk about the sex. Just, please, never call a woman's vagina a 'lady taco' again."

I lean over and pour some more wine into her glass, earning me a grateful smile.

I think I like book club.

An incessant knocking drags me to the surface of my unconscious state the next morning. My head hurts, my throat is fuzzy, and I can't remember how I got home last night. Not only did we drink both bottles of wine

I brought for book club, but we also managed to go through two more bottles that Paige had. Makes me wonder how Mila fared getting up early to open the bakery today.

I drag myself up and out of bed, and stumble to the door, squinting against the light stabbing my eyes. When I open it, I actually think I'm still asleep at first. Why else would Ethan be standing at my door, looking even more impossibly handsome than I remember? This has to be a dream. I close the door, then open it again. Nope, he's still there, raising his eyebrow at me like he can't figure out what's wrong with me.

"You're not supposed to be here," I state, rubbing my face to make sure I am, indeed, awake.

"Surprise?" he says, only it comes out as a question. "I decided to get up early and drive home. Partly so I can get a day in at the office catching up on things, but mostly because I missed you." He drops his gaze to the floor at that last part, and I see his cheeks turn pink.

Right as I'm about to launch myself into his arms, headache be damned, I freeze. If I look half as bad as I feel, then this is not good. Not good at all. He's still out in the hallway, so I slam the door shut on him for the second time, only this time I yell through the door, "Hang on."

I hear a soft thud and then his resigned voice, muffled by the door. "Not going anywhere, shorty."

I walk as quickly as my pounding head will allow into the bathroom, pop a couple of pain killers, splash cold water on my face, and brush my teeth. My hair is magically not that offensive, so I finger comb it and leave it. The torn T-shirt and pajama shorts with penguins on them have got to go, and I pull on a pair of soft leggings and an oversized sweater that hangs off one shoulder. A swipe of lip balm and that's as good as I'm going to get at nine am with a hangover. Wait. Nine am? Jeez, I haven't slept this late in years. No wonder I'm groggy.

I make my way back to the front door and open it once more to find Ethan leaning against the wall opposite my apartment.

"Hi."

He pushes off the wall and walks over to me, not stopping until he's pushed me back into my apartment. He kicks the door shut, takes my face gently in his hands, and brushes his lips softly over my forehead.

"If you're feeling as rough as my sister seems to be this morning, I'll be gentle. But I need to kiss you, Summer. Please tell me I can kiss you."

"Yes, please," I breathe, and that's all I can get out before his mouth is on mine. Our kiss turns into a frenzy, and I walk him over to the couch, pushing him down before straddling his lap. My hands go to the hem of his shirt and I impatiently tug at it until he pulls it off over his head. I let out a noise of satisfaction as my fingers roam his chest, reacquainting myself with the feel of his skin, the smattering of hair and the ripples of his muscles.

"Did you just purr?" He pulls back, his abs rippling with laughter under my hands.

"No," I say indignantly.

"Yeah, you did."

"I..."

"Maybe I should call you kitten."

"Don't you dare!" I slap at his chest lightly, and he growls, grabbing my hand and holding it in place. I lean down and kiss him again, letting my mouth travel from his lips to his jaw, over to his ear, and down his neck. He moves his fingers up my sides slowly, grazing over my body and making me shiver. He sweeps my hair over one shoulder and presses a kiss to the skin he bares.

"I love this tattoo. It's perfect for you. Beautiful, unique, strong." His fingers graze what he can reach of it.

"Mmm hmm," I mumble, tipping my head to the side and twisting so he can see all of it. *Take my shirt off. Please take my shirt off.* I silently beg, but he doesn't listen.

"Tell me about it?" he asks, almost conversationally, and I want to growl with frustration.

"Your self-control is kind of driving me crazy, Ethan," I pout.

He laughs and drops his forehead down to my shoulder. "It's killing me, trust me. I want to flip you over the back of this couch, strip these leggings off of you and slide into you. But I promised you a date first."

"The date that feels like it will never come," I grumble half heartedly. The truth is, I think it's unbelievably sweet and romantic that he's insisting on a proper date before we let things go too far.

"It's coming. Tonight. And after, you will be, too." He smacks one more kiss on my lips before lifting me off his lap, standing, and walking over to the door. "But if I don't get to the office and tackle the massive amount of inane paperwork that I'm positive awaits me, I won't get home in time to make dinner. See you at six?"

I nod, a stupid smile on my face. Ethan winks, then leaves. Don't get me wrong, I'm thrilled he stopped by, I really did miss him. But Goddamnit, must I always be left so freaking frustrated?

A few minutes before six, I knock on his door nervously. I love Ethan's house; last time I was here, I couldn't help but notice that the style is exactly what I always wanted in my own dream house. It's Craftsman style, which I only know because of the time that I was recovering from dental surgery and spent way too many hours daydreaming over houses and reading home design magazines nonstop. The wide porch has a swing on it, a real honest-to-goodness porch swing. White columns frame the stairs leading up to the door, and windows let in plenty of light. A large dormer hints at an upstairs room, but I haven't seen that much. Mila mentioned that when he bought it, the house was a dump. It certainly isn't anymore. Even the garden seems well-kept, with tidy flower beds and a paved walkway leading up to the front porch.

When the door opens, my breath catches in my throat. He's wearing a dark grey, long-sleeve Henley that molds to the contours of his body perfectly, jeans, and his feet are bare. Good God, why are men so damn sexy when they have bare feet? His hair is damp, and I can smell the scent of what I assume is his soap or shampoo. Citrusy, fresh, delicious.

"Come here," he practically growls, grabbing my arm and pulling me inside and straight into his arms. With his hands resting on my lower back, and our pelvises lined up, he peppers my skin with light kisses, dancing around my cheeks until finally landing on my mouth. My fingers find their way into his hair, holding him, fusing him to my lips.

"Want to put bets on what interrupts us tonight? Could be your sister, a town emergency, earthquake, UFO sighting," I tease, but my words end with a shriek as Ethan picks me up and tosses me over his shoulder, his hand coming down to smack me lightly on my ass.

"Fuck it. We're skipping dinner. I want dessert first."

Chapter 14

Ethan

It would take a disaster of monumental size to tear me away from Summer right now. We've waited too fucking long for this and I'll be damned if I'm going to let one more thing stand in the way of us being together.

We reach my bedroom, and I set her down gently on her feet before stepping back and quickly shucking my shirt and pants. The way she's watching me has my dick hardening, straining against the confines of my boxer briefs. I reach for her and lift the hem of her sweater, taking it gently over her head, watching the cascade of her hair as it falls free. The dark green bra she's wearing makes my mouth water as I envision what lies beneath.

I need to slow down. Savor this. Somehow, I force my hands to steady, reaching for her pants and slowly lowering them over her hips. Her panties match the bra, and I can feel my pulse thundering in my veins.

I knew she had the lotus blossom tattooed on her shoulder, but now I can also see a line of script on her hip. My fingers go to trace the words, *strong enough.* She certainly is. This magnificent woman is stronger than anyone I know.

"You're fucking gorgeous, Summer." My voice sounds hoarse, full of the arousal I've had to keep at bay all week.

"Ethan," there is a plea in her voice that my body responds to automatically. God, the things that makes me want to do to her. I want to hear her call out my name over and over as I drive her over the edge of sanity with orgasms. And I want it now.

I push her backward until she lands on the edge of my bed, then I drop to my knees in front of her. When my fingers hook into the edge of her panties, she lifts her hips eagerly. Yeah, she's as ready for this as I am. But I take my time, teasing her as I slowly drag them down her legs. Then just as slowly, I drag my fingers up her legs, until I reach her knees. That's when my self-control snaps. I push her legs open and place my mouth on her.

I press kisses to her mound, then open my mouth letting my tongue swipe up her length. She's sweet, honey sweet, and slightly musky. I could get drunk on the taste of her. Her hands are tangled in my hair, holding my head right where she wants me. Not that I would move from this spot before she comes. No fucking way.

Her hips start to buck against my face as I suck on her clit; her moans are getting louder. My cock is throbbing, begging to be set free, but I know that once I slide into her heat, I won't last long. And she needs at least two orgasms before that happens.

I quickly dart my tongue in and out, swirling around her clit, alternating between licking and sucking until her body goes rigid.

"Oh God, Ethan, oh my God!" she moans as her body lets go. But I'm not done. Even as her taste is drenching my tongue, I keep sucking, and slowly slide two fingers inside.

"Oh, *fuck*," Summer cries out, her hands pulling my hair harder. The pain only adds to the overwhelming sensations coursing through my body — ecstasy, lust, and an insatiable drive to keep bringing her all the pleasure I can.

Suddenly the grip on my hair loosens, and I glance up to see her gripping the sheets beside her, her back arched, putting her tits on a spectacular display. But my hands are too busy to reach up and grab them. My fingers are being squeezed by her tight core and my other palm is holding her hip in place as she thrusts up to meet my mouth.

I keep going until her body finally stops shuddering. Only then do I slowly kiss my way up her stomach, stopping at her lace covered breasts. I tug the cups of her bra down, freeing her nipples, and suck one into my mouth, then the other. She arches up and reaches behind herself to undo her bra and toss it away, and I grin at her as my hands cup her tits together.

"You blow my mind when you come," I say, my voice a low rumble even to my ears.

"Then make me come again," she says, her eyes alight with fire and passion.

"Gladly."

I surge up and kiss her lips; her groan when she tastes herself on my mouth is hot as fuck. Her hand slips down between our bodies and she grabs my cock, stroking it a few times.

"Shit. Condom." I sit back on my heels, my chest heaving up and down with the force it took to stop before it's too late.

"Hurry," Summer gasps.

I reach over to the side table, open a drawer, and grab the condom I pulled out of the brand-new box earlier. Buying those today was a hassle, seeing as I had to drive to Westport to get them. No privacy in a small town, which means someone would have seen me get them at the local drug store and rumours would have spread. I tear open the package with my teeth and quickly roll the latex over my dick. Then, leaning forward again, I notch my tip inside of her opening. A couple of shallow thrusts to ease her open, then she grabs my ass and pulls me forward until I'm balls deep inside of her.

She lets out a moan of satisfaction, and I drop my forehead down beside her. "Fucking hell, Summer. Finally."

I start to move my hips, slowly in and out, grunting every time the tip of my cock hits her inner wall. Her fingers are digging into my back and her heels are pushing into the bed, lifting her hips to meet my thrusts. Somehow, we find our rhythm, coming together perfectly in sync. I sense my orgasm is close, but I'll be damned if I come before she does again.

"Come for me, Summer. Let me feel you," I rasp in her ear just as she grabs my face and pulls my lips to meet hers. I watch her cheeks turn pink and her breath speeds up as she starts to keen, then cry out my name.

"Ethan, oh shit, yes, there. Right there. Oh, oh yes, yes!"

Her voice echoes not only around the room but in my heart as I let go inside of her. Her walls are clenching around me, squeezing every last drop of release out of me. The power of my orgasm is unrelenting and seems to go on forever. But eventually, I slow down. I keep on leisurely sliding in and out of her, prolonging both of our pleasure, but my arms are shaking, and I know I can't hold myself up for long. She just feels too damn good. But eventually I pull out of her and hop off the bed, walking over to the bathroom where I deal with the condom. When I get back to the bed, she's laying on her side, her head propped on her hand. The sheet is pooled around her waist, and I can see the curve of her breasts, tempting me. Fucking hell, she looks good in my bed. I could easily let myself want to see her there every goddamn night. I slide under the sheet next to her and gather her in my arms. We spend a minute or two lying there silently, before Summer lifts up slightly, keeping her eyes faced down at my chest.

"I want to say that was worth waiting for, because it was." She pauses, then tilts her head to look at me with a smile that can only be described as pure mischief. "But I'm also mad as hell that I had to wait so long to experience it."

I laugh and pull her back down to my side. "You've got that right. Don't worry, we'll make up for lost time." But before I can make good on that statement, my stomach lets out a loud grumble.

"Okay, we'll make up for lost time *after* dinner."

My arm is weighed down by something warm, and it takes me several minutes to figure out what that is as I slowly wake the next morning. The next thing that hits me is the smell of Summer's shampoo, from her hair that is spread over my pillow. Lavender. Peppermint. I slowly slide my arm out from underneath her so I can prop up on my elbow and watch her sleep.

Last night was amazing. There's no other word for it. Well, maybe life-altering, mind-blowing, intense, best sex ever. Yeah. Those words work, too.

Summer rolls over, mumbling in her sleep. I carefully tuck some hair behind her ear, earning a soft sigh. I lean down and kiss her cheek, letting my lips trace across her skin lightly. A whisper of a caress that leaves me hungry for more. I press my lips to her face again, this time closer to the corner of her mouth. When she stirs, I move down her neck, brushing over her collarbone. When she shifts onto her back, her hand coming up to cup my head, I grin.

"Morning, shorty," I whisper against the top of her breast.

"Mmmmph."

"Not awake yet?" I look up at her. Her eyes are tightly shut but there's a smile dancing on her lips. She shakes her head slowly. My mouth returns to my exploration of her body, landing on her breast. I gently suck her nipple into my mouth, teasing the tip into a hard nub. She arches into me, with a moan that stirs some primal need in me to claim this woman as mine.

"How about now?" I murmur.

She shakes her head again, only this time her smile is bigger. This playful side of Summer might be my favourite. Chuckling, I return to what I was doing, making my way down her body, letting my tongue trace circles over her stomach while my hands stay up on her breasts, squeezing them gently.

"Ethan," she rasps. Her voice is laden with sleep and lust and my already rigid cock twitches against my leg. She must feel it because her foot draws a line up my leg to tease me, wrapping around my waist with her heel digging in right below my ass.

"I'm starving for you, Summer," I say, lifting my head to see her watching me, her eyes heavy with arousal.

"Then have me."

I reach over for the package of condoms, but the box is empty. "Shit. We used all of the condoms last night."

Summer arches her brow. "Guess you should've bought the bigger box."

I roll onto my back, chuckling. "Well, to be fair, three times in one night is a new record for me. That, and they didn't have a bigger box at the store."

She giggles at that, before sitting up, swinging her legs over the side of the bed and looking over her shoulder at me. My hand drifts up to stroke her bare back and she arches slightly into my touch.

"You know what doesn't need a condom?"

I move beside her, my gaze drifting down to where her breasts are bare. "What?"

"Blow jobs in the shower."

Before I can even process a response, she's jumped out of bed and is running and giggling into the bathroom. My brain catches up to what she said, and I stand up and stalk after her. When I get to the bathroom, it's already filling with steam, and she's in the shower. I open the glass door and step in with her. Thank God I installed a large shower stall when I renovated the bathroom. That was fucking genius of me.

Summer holds my gaze as she drops down to her knees. The water is streaming over both of us, and I close my eyes, tipping my face up. She wastes no time taking me in her hands, squeezing the base of my dick, and I slap the wall of the shower in front of me.

"Fuck."

I look down, just in time to see her open her mouth and take me inside. I bite back my moan as her tongue swirls around my tip, but when she hollows her mouth and sucks my length in, I grunt and my abs contract. My breath speeds up as she works me with her mouth and her hands. I can feel my balls tighten and part of me wonders at the fact that this woman can drive me to climax so goddamn quickly. She's got a direct line to my orgasms and knows how to bring one on in minutes. If I wasn't confident that I can repay that favour tenfold, I'd be worried.

But there's no time to overthink things, not when Summer brings her other hand around from where it was cupping my ass and starts to fondle my balls.

"Summer. Holy shit, Summer. I'm gonna come, babe."

She hums, and the sound vibrates on my dick. That's all it takes, and I hunch over as my orgasm rips through me. I shoot into her mouth, shouting something as she swallows it down. I have no fucking clue what I say; I'm oblivious to anything but my climax until I'm spent.

Slowly she slides up my body, coming to stand in between my arms which are still stretched out in front of me, using the wall to hold me up. She kisses me, and even though I can taste myself on her lips, I don't give a fuck. I kiss her greedily, trying to pour everything I'm feeling, even the stuff I don't quite understand yet, into that kiss.

"Thank you," I say, before taking my bar of soap and running it over her body, letting the suds smooth the way for my fingers to dance over her body. But when I reach between her legs and play with her clit, she shifts back, an apologetic smile on her face.

"I think I might need a little break, actually. You're not the only one who isn't used to three rounds in one night."

I chuckle softly, letting my hands move to her hips before leaning in and kissing her lightly.

"No problem. Can't have you too sore for tonight."

"What's tonight?" she asks.

"I thought we might try for four."

Sitting beside Summer, eating eggs and toast, is the most domestic thing I've ever done with any woman. And I fucking love every second of it. When it's finally time for her to go, we linger in the front entryway, kissing goodbye.

"I have to go, Ethan," she smiles against my lips. "Besides, I'll see you later for the work party."

"Maybe we should just stay here. What if someone sees you leave," I tease as my lips travel down her neck. She moans with pleasure and pushes weakly on my shoulders.

"They've probably already noticed my truck parked out front all night," she says, and pulls my face back up to hers. "We have to tell Mila about us."

I drop my forehead to hers. "We do."

"Soon." Summer kisses me one more time, then leaves me standing there, already missing her.

Just over an hour later, I finish up a punishing ten kilometer run with a walk down Main Street to cool down. On impulse, I decide to stop in and see Mila. Sunday mornings are normally busy for her, but I must have caught her in a weird lull because when I walk in, there's no one in the café except Mila, who I can see in the back, and the girl who's working the cash register.

"Hey big brother," she calls out cheerily. "Grab some coffee, I'll bring out fresh muffins in a minute."

I do just that, pouring a coffee from the self-serve carafes and head over to my favourite chair to wait for my sister.

She comes over a few minutes later with a plate holding two muffins.

"You look way too stressed out for this early in the morning. When was the last time you got laid?"

I can feel the heat instantly flooding my face. Shit. Does Mila know? "What? I..." I try to think of a response quickly, but Mila laughs, waving me off.

"I'm kidding, big brother. I don't want to know a single thing about your love life. Got it?"

A customer walks in and Mila stands up to go help them. Midway across the bakery, she turns back to me.

"But I know Summer means more to you than just a friend, Ethan, I'm not blind. And if you hurt her, I'll have to kill you."

Chapter 15

Summer

MILA: Hope you're ready for the work party this afternoon! Meet me at the bakery at two and we can go over to the resort together.

Mila's text came through sometime last night, probably in between my second and third orgasm. I'm glad I didn't check my phone until now, when I'm at home alone, because the instant guilt I feel seeing her name is hard to handle. Last night was spectacular; I'm pretty sure I am still vibrating from every incredible climax Ethan brought me to. I want to be able to share how happy I am with my best friend, but she doesn't even know I'm with someone. Much less that the someone is her brother.

SUMMER: Awesome! See you later.

I hit send on my reply and drop my phone down on the counter before slumping down on one of the chairs. I hate lying. Almost as much as I hate being lied to. I guess I just have to hope that Mila can accept Ethan and I being together, because right now there's not much that could make me walk away from him.

Waking up this morning in Ethan's arms was pure heaven. I was filled with an overwhelming sense of being right where I belonged. It was so intense that it almost brought a tear to my eye. He may have thought I was still sleeping while he kissed his way across my body, but the truth is, I knew the moment he woke up. My body was so in tune with his that my subconscious mind knew he was awake long before my conscious mind caught up to the way he was teasing me.

Heaving a sigh, I get up and get started on my laundry and other mundane chores that need to happen. At least the jobs serve to keep me slightly distracted, so I don't waste the entire morning daydreaming about Ethan. But around lunchtime, the lack of sleep from last night catches up to me and I find myself yawning over and over. I decide to lay down for a while, hoping that a short nap will help me be ready for this afternoon.

The obnoxious sound of my phone alarm going off on the pillow beside me wakes me from a hot dream involving Ethan and whipped cream. But when I blink bleary eyed at the screen to see that it's already after two, I spring up, fumbling to find a sweater and socks. *Shit*. I hate being late. I hurry down the stairs, thankful that the bakery is literally right beneath me. All the same, when I pull the door open, I'm full of apology. "Oh God, I am so freaking sorry! I laid down and must have fallen asleep," I say, and Mila looks up from the counter where she seems to be inspecting something closely.

"First of all, you're like, five minutes late. No big deal. Second, coffee?" She walks over to the espresso maker and starts it up without even waiting for my response.

"You're a goddess," I groan, walking forward and sinking into a chair. While she's busy, my phone buzzes with another text.

A couple of minutes later, Mila walks over with a steaming cup of caffeinated delight, and even the aroma is enough to perk me up. Then she turns back to the counter and picks something up before coming and sitting down across from me.

"Feel free to call me a goddess on a daily basis," she says cheerily, sliding a plate in front of me. "Now, try this, and be honest."

I eye the plate curiously. There's a delicate looking pastry on it that reminds me of those hasselback potatoes that were huge several years ago, only better, and covered with icing sugar. "What is it?"

"Sfogliatella."

"Foggy what now?"

Mila laughs. "Sfogliatella. It's an Italian pastry. I've been experimenting with flavors for a couple of weeks now, and I think I finally have something worth adding to the menu. This one has an orange mascarpone filling between the layers."

I bite into the flaky pastry and sweet citrus notes explode on my tongue along with the buttery taste of the pastry and the richness of the mascarpone. "Oh my God, this is incredible." Crumbs fly out of my mouth and I don't even care as I take another bite. "I'm gonna need another one."

Mila's shoulders are back, and her eyes gleam with pride. "That's exactly what I wanted to hear." She stands and goes back to the kitchen, returning with two more pastries.

"Gimme, gimme, gimme. Just don't expect me to ever say the name right," I say, reaching for one. My eyes close as I bite down. It really is sinfully delicious.

After I finish my second pastry in record time, I lean back, holding my cup of coffee that sadly pales in comparison to the delicious treat I just ate. *Sorry, coffee, you can't compete with foggy-whatever it's called.*

"Mom used to tease Dad that the way to his heart was through his stomach," Mila says fondly. "Funny how I can bake up a storm but can't find a man. Curse of living in a small town, I guess."

It's the first time I've heard Mila mention her love life, and my ears perk up. "There's got to be some eligible bachelors in town."

She snorts. "Umm, nope. None that I would be interested in, at least. The only remotely attractive one would be Reid, but I've known him for way too long. I had to suffer through his emo punk phase when he and Ethan were teenagers. How the school ever got over that enough to hire him as principal I will never understand." She lets out a loud sigh. "If I'm going to live in Dogwood Cove, I'm going to live a spinster. And since I wouldn't be able to afford a bakery anywhere else, I guess I better start my cat collection."

"Aren't you allergic to cats?"

Mila shrugs. "Fine. I'll collect dogs."

I roll my eyes at that. "Mila, you work ridiculous hours at a bakery. Collecting animals doesn't seem like a viable option."

"Stop shooting down my ideas, Summer. Just because you're happy in a relationship, doesn't mean the rest of us will be so lucky."

And there it is.

"So, you know about Ethan and I," I say nervously, my hands clutching my coffee cup tightly.

"Well, I do now that you confirmed it," she answers, and I venture a glance up to gauge her reaction. She doesn't seem mad.

"I'm sorry we didn't tell you; it was my idea not to. I wasn't sure how you'd feel."

"Not gonna lie, it's weird. And it does suck that you didn't feel like you could tell me. But if you like him that way, and he likes you, I guess I can't stand in the way." She shrugs, as if it's no big deal. Meanwhile, my heart is pounding. "Just don't tell me any details about your sex life, okay? I love you both, but eww. No thanks." Mila shudders. Then her lips curl up into a smile. "And hey, if you marry him, we'll be sisters." Mila says impishly.

I can't help it, I burst out laughing. "How about we go on more than one date before you start planning our wedding?"

Mila chuckles at that, but then her expression turns serious.

"Speaking seriously, Summer, I'm okay with you guys getting together. Just promise me you'll tell me if he hurts you so I can kick his ass."

I feel more freaking tears start to build. "Thanks, Mila."

"Chicks before dicks. Sisters before misters. Friends before men." Mila raises her coffee cup and we cheer each other. Then her face and her tone sobers. "But Summer, don't hurt him either, okay?"

My brows pull together in confusion. "I wasn't planning on it."

Mila nods, her eyes downcast. "Look, it probably isn't my business, but I know my brother won't talk about it. A few years ago, not long after Mom and Dad died, he had his heart broken. She was a teacher, here on contract. Even though her job wasn't permanent, she made him believe that she would stay. Then two weeks before her contract was up, she told him she had accepted a job on the mainland. He tried to convince everyone that it was no big deal, but I know my brother. He's got a huge heart full of love to give, and she broke it."

I'm silent after she finishes, processing what she's told me. Even though I have no intention of hurting Ethan, I can read between the lines. Mila's worried that if I leave, it'll hurt Ethan. I guess I need to make it clear that I don't plan on leaving.

"Thanks for telling me, Mila," I say quietly.

She gives me a small smile in return. "Okay, enough drama. Are you ready for this work party? I think there should be about six of us ready to work for a few hours, so we had better get out there and get started."

My heart warms at that. All of these people coming together to help me. Mila might complain about a lack of eligible men in a small town, but even she has to see the benefit of living somewhere that everyone comes together to help those in need. Even if the person in need hasn't lived there for almost two decades.

We climb into my truck, Mila setting a large box filled with what I hope are more pastries on the back seat, and set off for the short drive to the resort. When we arrive, there are already several cars parked. I can see Ethan standing with a group of people and he seems to be giving directions.

"He can't help but put himself in charge," Mila huffs.

"It's probably a good thing. After all, it's not as if I know much about renovations," I say.

She turns to me and reaches one hand out to rest on my leg. "I'm really glad you're doing this, Summer. You can reopen this place, better than it ever was. I believe that."

That's exactly what I needed to hear right now, as the massive amount of work to be done at the resort is looming in front of me. Even with all of these people here to help, I know it's going to take weeks, maybe even months, to get close to operational. Not to mention all of the money I still need to magically find.

"Do you really think I can?" I ask quietly, staring out the front window at Ethan who has noticed our arrival, and is walking over. "The other day I was thinking about selling. Even if I can't get much for it, at least then I wouldn't have the stress of wondering how I'll ever make it work."

When I glance over at Mila, she looks guilty. And nervous. Before I can ask her what's wrong, my door opens, and Ethan's voice fills the cab.

"There's my two favourite ladies, I was wondering when you would get here."

I turn to him quickly and smile, climbing down from my truck. His gaze darts between me and Mila, filled with uncertainty, so I rise up on my toes to kiss him.

"She knows, and it's fine."

"Thank fuck," he murmurs against my lips.

"Alright, alright. Break it up you two. Just because I'm okay with this doesn't mean I want to see it all the time. Got it?" Mila pushes between us, taking me by the arm and tugging me away from Ethan. Once she has us separated, she faces us, her hands on her hips.

Mila looks back and forth between us for a minute, and I swear to God she's purposefully drawing this out to make me go crazy.

"Alright, here's how this is going to work." She points her finger at Ethan first. "You hurt my best friend or make her want to leave town, and I'll disown you." Ethan coughs back a laugh, but when Mila glowers at him, he nods. My heart is racing now, wondering what the heck she's going to say to me.

"And as for you, missy." The finger is pointed in my direction now. "He's my brother. I don't want to hear any details about anything. You understand me?" Ethan doesn't even bother to try and cover his snort of laughter now, but instead of glowering, Mila just rolls her eyes at him before turning back to me.

"We're best friends, Summer. He might be my brother, and I can't help but love him, but as I said before, chicks before dicks." She dusts her hands together. "So, you're dating. And we'll all be adults about this, and you two will not hurt each other, or put me in the middle of anything. Deal?"

"Deal," I say quickly, relieved she took it so well.

"Can't believe you've managed to make this all about you," Ethan grumbles, and I shove him in the side with my elbow. "Oww. Geez, shorty, those elbows are pointy." He rubs his side, pouting at me.

"Your sister is okay with us dating. Let it go, lumberjack."

"Oh God, that's the perfect nickname." Mila snickers. "Okay, moving on. Work party time."

And with that, Ethan takes my hand and steers us toward the group of people. "Come and meet your labourers for the day, Summer."

When we reach everyone, he does a quick round of introductions. Aside from him and Mila, Paige and Reid are here, also, and I shoot them both a grateful smile. There are also two older men standing next to Reid. They introduce themselves as Turner and Pete, and Ethan explains that Turner owns the hardware store, and Pete is a mechanic. I thank them both profusely for donating their Sunday afternoon to me, to which Pete chuckles.

"Any chance to get our hands dirty with some good old hard work is time well spent, girly. Besides, I remember your Daddy's big plans for this place. It sure would be nice to see it all done."

Turner nods in agreement. "Carl would be so happy to see you back here, working on the resort."

My eyes threaten to fill with tears. Ethan must see them because his arm around my shoulders tightens.

"Did you know my dad well?" I ask, hoping they say yes. What I wouldn't give to be able to talk to my dad's friends and find out what his life was like while I was gone.

"If you call weekly beers and having him kick my ass at pool 'knowing him well', then yes," Turner says with a sad smile. "Sandra and I would be happy to have you over for dinner sometime and fill you in on anything we can. He missed you something fierce."

Forget threatening to fill, now my eyes are overflowing. I can't formulate words, so all I do is nod. Ethan's there for me, however, just like always.

"That would be great, Turner, thank you. Maybe we can set something up before we finish today."

Ethan presses a kiss to the side of my head, right there in front of everyone. I gulp back my tears, sniffing loudly.

"Thank you, all of you, for coming to help. It really means so much to me that you're here and willing to help."

Ethan drops his arm to clap his hands together. "Okay, so everyone knows what job they are starting with. The focus of today is mostly cleanup, but if you finish your assigned cabin or area and want more to do, just find me. I'll be working with Summer on cabin number one."

Everyone smiles, and the group breaks apart, leaving Ethan and I standing alone. I'm filled with such an immense amount of gratitude for him, Mila, and this whole damn town.

I wrap my arms around his middle and hug him tightly. "Thank you," I mumble against his chest, feeling him chuckle in response.

"We all want to help you, Summer." He bends down and presses a kiss to my head before leaning down to whisper. "I simply happen to want to *help* you in more ways than just here at the resort." He pulls back and winks before taking my hand and leading me over to the first cabin. When we get there, he bends down and picks up a tool belt with a hammer hanging from it and attaches it around my waist. Then he stands back and grins.

"Ready to work?"

Chapter 16

Ethan

Even though I do my best to keep a cheerful and encouraging perspective all afternoon, it doesn't reflect the churning emotions I'm facing on the inside. Summer's pain when she heard Pete and Turner talk about her dad is eating away at me.

With the perspective I have now, I can appreciate the sad look that was often on Carl's face at family events like the summer solstice festival, the fall fair, and the Christmas tree lighting. He was missing his daughter, the same way she is missing him now. I get the sense that she sees Oceanside as her last tie to him, and while that gives me hope that she would never want to sell, I can't underestimate the financial strain this place puts on her.

It's early evening, we've been working for several hours, and things are looking good. Mila had everyone organized into groups, tackling as much cleanup as we could get done in the time we had. The list of renovations that have to be done next is daunting to me, so I can't imagine how Summer is feeling. But she's in a better mood now, thanks in part to me sneaking kisses every chance I get.

Like right now. Holding her flush against my body, tasting the bead of sweat on her upper lip. Kissing her makes me feel as if I'm drowning and coming up for air all at the same damn time.

"Hello? Mayor Monroe? Hello?"

We break apart, and I look down at Summer, confused as to who is calling my name. Not many people bother calling me Mayor Monroe, I'm simply Ethan. Then I hear Mila's voice chime in.

"Mrs. Henderson, so nice of you to stop by."

"Hattie Henderson is still alive?" Summer whispers to me, and I fight to hold in my laughter.

"She's gonna outlive us all," I whisper back. "I better go and see why she's here."

I make my way out of the cabin we've been working on, brushing my hands on my pants as I go.

"Hello, Mrs. Henderson. What brings you to Oceanside?" I ask cordially.

"I'm here for Carl's girl. She's the one running this place now, isn't she?"

I nod, still confused, as Summer comes up to stand beside me.

"Hello, I'm Summer Harris."

"Yes, dear, I know. I used to babysit you when you were an infant. I'd recognize those blue-green eyes anywhere."

"Wh...what? You did? I don't...I don't remember that." Summer stammers, her hand blindly grabbing for mine. I take it and link our fingers together, feeling her surprise and confusion mirroring mine.

"Oh yes. Your father, rest his soul, would sometimes have to go looking for that woman who birthed you. She was always off gallivanting in the city. Carl would call me, and I'd sit with you at night."

Summer sways, and my arm automatically comes around her. Mila and Serena are standing close by, listening to everything, but the others are still working. No one brings any attention to the way Mrs. Henderson describes Summer's mom, but the biting tone makes it clear what the old lady thought of her.

"Mrs. Henderson, I think it's safe to say Summer is a bit confused by what you're telling her. Could you possibly explain?"

Hattie Henderson, who most of my generation know as the kooky lady who wears a fancy hat to go to the grocery store, pats Summer's arm kindly.

"Of course, of course. I'm sorry, dear." She shuffles over to a chair someone put out and sinks down into it. "Your mother was never happy here. Did you know the story of how your parents met?" She looks up at Summer, who shakes her head. Mila brings over another chair, and with a grateful smile, Summer sits down. I bring my hand to her shoulder, to let her know I'm still here.

"Well. Carl told me all about it one evening when he asked me over to watch you. He was so exhausted from trying to keep that woman happy; he just couldn't take it any longer and needed to tell someone. Poor soul. From what he said, it seems he met your mother at a music festival in Vancouver. She got pregnant that night, and he wanted to do right by the two of you. So, when he asked her to move here with him, she agreed. But that woman wasn't made for small town life. She missed the hustle and bustle of the city and was often picking up and leaving town for a day or two. But with no such thing as cell phones back then, well, she'd send your father into a right state when she would disappear."

I swear if my arms weren't holding Summer up, she would have collapsed to the ground. It's clear this is all coming as a total shock for her. Part of me is glad we might be getting some insight into her mother, but I can see how hard this is for her as well. I ache to take away the pain and comfort her. And I will, later.

"This went on for over three years. Carl would call me; I lived right next door you see, and I would look after you while he would go and find your mother. Then one night, something happened. He never did tell me exactly what, but he came home with bruised knuckles and a much more subdued version of your mother." At Summer's intake of breath, Mrs. Henderson shakes her head and taps her knee. "Oh, no, no, no, dear, he didn't hurt her. He hurt someone, certainly, but never your mother. Despite everything, he loved her dearly. Almost as much as he loved you. She didn't ever disappear again after that night, but I know your father was very stressed. Always worried she would leave again, and that someday she would take you with her. And then one day, of course, she did." Mrs. Henderson's eyes start to water. "He was heartbroken. I asked why he never went after you, and that's when he told me he couldn't. He said your mother promised to let you come home if you ever asked to, and when you never did, he assumed it was your choice."

"It wasn't. I never knew he wanted me, she never told me anything," Summer blurts out, her voice shaking. She turns and buries her face in my stomach, sobs wracking her body. Out of the corner of my eye, I see Mila and Serena go to Mrs. Henderson and comfort her, but she brushes them off and stands, walking over to us. Her eyes meet mine, and I see nothing but care and affection in them, so I let her turn Summer to face her.

"Summer, your father was like the son I never had. I won't speak ill of your mother, because without her, we wouldn't have you. He loved you, and so did I. And I know that he's so happy you are finally home."

I watch, helpless as Summer stands up and folds herself into Mrs. Henderson's arms. It's clear that both women cared about Carl very much from the way the two hold each other, lost in their own grief and sadness. Serena and Mila go back to work, giving them some privacy, but there's no way I'm leaving.

Eventually, Mrs. Henderson steps back, patting Summer on the arms. "There's so much more I want to talk to you about, my dear. But not today. For now, I just needed to get a good look at you, and at the resort. Carl had such plans for this place."

"I'd love to show you around," Summer says, a watery smile on her beautiful, tear-streaked face. I watch the two of them walk away, stopping to greet Pete and Turner, before carrying on for a slow walk around the property.

"Who would have guessed Mrs. Henderson would have all the intel on Summer's childhood."

Mila comes to stand beside me.

"No shit. I wonder what else she knows," I mutter under my breath, before turning to my sister. "How are things going in the main building?"

"Great, actually. We got a first coat of paint done everywhere. There's a few loose floorboards to deal with, but it's pretty much a blank slate in there now."

"That's fantastic. Thanks, Mills."

Mila shoves at me with her shoulder. "She may be your girlfriend, but she's my best friend. I want to see her happy just as much as you do."

Serena joins us then. "I'm going to head out, guys. I've got a class to prepare for."

"Thanks for coming Serena," I flash her a grateful smile. "I'll tell Summer you had to go."

Serena waves, and walks to her car. Reid, Turner, and Pete come up to us not long after.

"Well, son, I think we got some mighty good work done today," Turner says, wiping his brow with a cloth. "Carl would be damn happy to see this place coming together."

"Muffins are on me tomorrow, okay guys? I'll save you some apple streusel ones," Mila says, earning her a round of thanks.

Reid claps me on the shoulder. "I'm off, too, need to prep some stuff before work tomorrow."

"See ya man, thanks for helping out."

Summer and Mrs. Henderson make their way back to us just as Reid is pulling out.

"Oh shoot, did I miss getting to say goodbye and thank you to everyone?" she says, showing off her gigantic, caring heart once again.

"Don't worry. They know you're grateful," I reassure her.

"Mrs. Henderson, can I trouble you for a ride back into town? I don't think Ethan and Summer are quite ready to go yet, and I need to get some prep work done at the bakery." My sister winks at me as she takes the old lady's arm.

"Thank you so much for coming and telling me about my dad," Summer interjects.

Mrs. Henderson gives her a meaningful smile, and I get the idea that the two of them spoke about a lot of things on their walk around the resort. "Don't forget to come and see me soon, dear. There's so many more things I want to tell you."

As we watch Mila and Mrs. Henderson go, Summer puts her arm around my waist and leans into my side with a soft sigh.

"Everything okay?" I ask.

"She lied to me. About so many things."

I know she's talking about her mother, and I know if I open my mouth right now all that will come out is anger at that woman.

"I've thought about calling her and asking why she did it. But I know she won't answer me, at least not with the truth. She'll tell me how terrible my father was, and how much she hated living here. She'll make it all about her. The same way she did everything when I was growing up." She turns to me, and the pain in her eyes spears my heart. "Why do people hide from the truth?"

"I wish I knew, babe. I'm so sorry." We stand there in silence for a while. I wish there was more that I could do right now, but there isn't. She's got to deal with the reality of what her mother kept from her. Eventually, the sky starts to darken, and I realize if I want to set up my surprise for her, I need to do it now.

"Why don't you move the chairs over to the spot in front of cabin one. We could build a fire and relax for a bit."

Summer looks up at me, and I'm relieved to see a small smile stretch across her face.

"That sounds wonderful."

I turn to gather some things from my truck while she moves the chairs. When I drop the pile of wood down beside the stone fire ring she's building, I whistle appreciatively. "Good to know you still remember how to do that."

Summer huffs out a laugh. "It's a circle of rocks, Ethan. Pretty sure it's a hard thing to forget." She stands up and brushes her hands together. "I'm going to disappear into the bushes for a minute. Be right back."

Fixing the plumbing in the cabin is our next priority. While she's gone, I quickly move the rest of my surprise into the cabin. It's a good thing we finished the work we were planning on doing today, or my surprise wouldn't work. Now I just hope she's into the idea. I set things up as quickly as I can, then shut the door to the cabin before Summer can get back.

When she returns, I've got the fire started, and have laid out some food.

"Hot dogs and s'mores?" she says with a laugh, sinking down into the chair next to mine.

"Perfect food for a campout at the beach, wouldn't you say?"

Her blinding smile shows no hint of her previous sadness, and I know without a doubt that I'll do anything on earth to make that happen again and again.

Chapter 17

Summer

"A campout?" I say, my heart filling with happiness that washes away the sadness from before. All thoughts of my mom's lies, or my dad's passing disappear.

Ethan looks at me, a grin stretching across his face. The flames from the fire dance on his skin, giving him a warm glow. "Yeah. You, me, a sleeping bag, a campfire, and the stars. Sound good?"

Chills dance over my skin, and not because it's cold.

"That sounds amazing," I whisper.

He rises out of his chair only to tug me out of mine and sit back down with me on his lap. His eyes penetrate me, seeing to the depths of my soul.

"Amazing is what you deserve, and more." This time when he kisses me, it's different. This isn't a kiss of passion or lust. This is a kiss of something deeper, more intense. This is a kiss of knowing, of seeing, of loving. His lips are promising forever, even if we haven't yet said the words. I don't need them, because I can sense what he isn't saying in his touch. I slant my mouth over his, eager to feel more of him, to send him the same unspoken message. Our tongues are dancing together, sliding over each other, as our hands grapple for an even stronger attachment.

When we break apart, we're both panting. I can feel his shoulders rising and falling underneath my touch, and the light from the campfire illuminates the lines of his jaw dusted with stubble; the shadows give him a dangerous air that is so at odds with the Ethan I know, the gentle lumberjack who feels so deeply.

"You look fierce and wild, like you might consume me."

Somehow his gaze both softens and grows more intense at the same time. His large hand comes up to cup the back of my neck, pulling our foreheads together so they touch.

"You *do* consume me."

His words wash over me, soft as silk sliding on my skin.

"Are you hungry, Summer?"

I shake my head. "Not for food."

In one swift move he stands and walks over to the cabin. At the door he pauses, and glances back at the fire.

"We can't leave that unattended," he says, his voice full of regret and indecision. "And once I get you inside, there's no way my attention will be anywhere but on you."

My inner vixen roars to life, giving me an idea. I push at him to get him to set me down. When he does, I take his hand and lead him back to the chairs by the fire. Slowly, I lift my shirt up and over my head. I see his eyes darken as he realizes what I'm up to. Then his shirt is off, and he's reaching for my pants, sliding them down my body, lowering himself to the ground. When he's on his knees in front of me, he stares up at me with reverence.

"Summer," he murmurs, and my heart seizes waiting to hear what he might say next. But no more words come. Instead of speaking, his mouth starts kissing. My stomach, my hips, the line where my skin meets my panties. Then his fingers are hooking in the sides of my underwear, and tugging them down, lifting my legs one by one to take them off. Everywhere his hands touch, his mouth follows, drawing lines and patterns up and down my legs until they are quivering so violently, I am certain I'll collapse.

The fire is slowly dying with no fresh wood being added, and the dimming light continues to trip across our skin, shining in parts and throwing shadows in others. Ethan stands, his gaze firmly planted on mine as he takes his jeans off. Then he sits down in a chair before guiding me to sit in his lap. His cock is straining upward, pushing against the fabric of his boxer briefs. I shift my hips slightly, freeing it and taking him in my hands. His head drops back, his mouth opening slightly, and I watch his Adam's apple bob up and down as he swallows. I lean in and lick up the line of his throat, feeling his cock throb in my palm in response.

"I want you, Ethan." I whisper against his neck.

"Then take me." He reaches down and pulls out a condom from his shorts. As soon as it's rolled on him, I use my hands to guide the tip of his cock to my entrance and slide down his length with a low moan. No one and nothing have ever filled me the way he does. I start to rock my hips as his hands come down to hold me. His fingers dig in, possessing me with his touch.

"Fucking hell, Summer," he rasps, his eyes drifting closed. My fingers are pressing into his chest, curled into the ropes of muscle that are straining with the passion that's overtaking us both. Whether it's the firelight, the sound of the waves, or the feel of Ethan, I sense my body taking over. I'm pulled by some unseen force into a rhythm that I don't control anymore. I give myself up to it, to him and to this moment. My senses are reduced to the warmth of his skin on mine, the sound of our moans and grunts as we come together thrust after thrust, and the fire building inside of me.

I lean forward to kiss him, needing his lips the way a junkie needs their next fix. I'm high on Ethan. He takes over, speeding us up, lifting my hips and slamming me back down on him. The sensation rides the fine line between pleasure and pain, hovering on the side of intense pleasure with perfect balance. He's claiming me with every thrust, his cock hitting my inner walls from every angle.

"You're perfect. This is perfect," he says, and his voice is filled with sensual wonder. "Fuck yes, God, shorty, you're squeezing me so tightly."

"Ethan," I gasp, tilting my hips forward so that every stroke of his cock hits me exactly where I need it.

The heat he is stoking inside of me is overwhelming my senses from the inside out, sending me higher than any human should possibly go. Any fear about the higher I climb, the further I fall, is fleeting at best, because I know he is right there with me, holding me, anchoring me to him. When we hurtle over the edge into ecstasy, we go together, clutching each other tightly. For several minutes we stay like that, tangled together, our hearts pounding in time. Eventually, Ethan's hands come up to brush the hair out of my face.

"When I said earlier that you consume me, I meant it. You've come back into my life and turned me inside out in the best possible way. I get lost in you, babe."

"That's okay. You can get lost. Because I found myself in you," I answer simply.

Ethan's hands still.

"Summer."

Then he kisses me again. And just like the kiss earlier, this one is laden with promises unspoken. Promises of forever, of love, of all the things I thought were impossible dreams.

Eventually hunger drives us to cook the hot dogs, turning the energy between us from romantic to playful. I've never had a boyfriend that I can have so much fun with. It's a layer of our relationship that I cherish almost as much as the more intimate moments. And after, Ethan pulls out the bag of marshmallows and we try to see who can roast the perfect one. When I lick marshmallow off of my fingers one by one, emphasizing the swirl of my tongue around the tip of my finger, his reaction is exactly what I hoped for.

"For fuck's sake, I'm never going to be able to eat s'mores again without getting a hard on," he growls, and I giggle.

"I'm not sorry for that," I tease. "You'll just have to never eat s'mores without me."

"Deal." He presses his lips against mine firmly, his tongue swiping at my upper lip. "Mmm. Sweet."

I lean my head down on his shoulder, and we sit there quietly watching the fire until it dies down again. Ethan tucks the blanket more securely around me.

"Do you want to go into the cabin?" he asks, and I shake my head.

"No, I want to look at the moon for a little while longer."

The silvery light reflecting on the water makes me realize I want a lifetime of moments like this. The peace and contentment that fills me, listening to the water lap against the shore, seeing the stars twinkling above us, this is what I've spent my life searching for and never finding. Eventually, the cold air seeps in and I start to shiver.

"Come on, shorty." Ethan kisses the top of my hair before standing up, still holding me, and carrying me, cradled into his arms toward the cabin. He kicks the door open before setting me down on my feet in the dark.

"Hang on." I hear him moving around, then one by one he turns on countless small LED candles until the cabin is bathed in a warm glow that mimics the fire we had outside.

"Oh, Ethan," I breathe. No one has ever done something so romantic, so thoughtful, for me. An air mattress is on the floor of the empty room, piled high with blankets and pillows, and the flickering lights are on every surface.

"Best part is, no raccoons," he says with a grin, kicking off his shoes and putting them by the door. "Come here." He holds his hand out to me, beckoning me closer. I take my shoes off as well before padding across the floor to him. I let him fold me into his strong embrace, breathing in the musky scent of him deeply. Together we lower down to the mattress. Ethan stretches out beside me, his fingers drifting in circles over my stomach and hips. His lips nip at my neck, licking and kissing a path down to my shoulder where he pulls down the hemline of my shirt to bare more skin. Earlier we were consumed with a frantic sort of passion, now it's more luxurious. We have nothing but time and each other.

I push him away, and we make quick work of our clothes. Then in the warmth of the nest of blankets he set up, Ethan makes me fly again and again.

Later, when I'm tucked into him, his chest pressed against my back as we cuddle together in the afterglow, he presses a kiss to my shoulder.

"Are you feeling better about the resort after today?"

I roll over in his arms so I can face him, bringing my hands underneath my head. He slides a leg in between mine so that we are still fully entwined in each other. I love the way he needs the connection just as much as I do.

"Yeah, I think I am," I reply. "There's still so much to do, but I'm starting to be able to see what this place will be eventually. I think...I think my dad would be happy," I say softly. Ethan leans forward and kisses a spot under my eyes that was damp with unshed tears.

"I know he would be."

The certainty in his voice makes me smile. I don't know how I got so lucky to have this man believe in me like he does. But I won't take a second of our time together for granted. Remembering what Mila told me about his ex, and how she up and left him with no warning, I pull him tighter. I don't think I could give this man up for anything.

Chapter 18

Ethan

We sleep soundly that night, tangled up in each other. And in the early morning light, Summer wakes me up by kissing her way down my chest and stomach. I flip her over onto her back, relishing her squeal of delight, and take my turn kissing and licking her body. She tastes salty and musky from our lovemaking last night, but perfectly feminine and fucking arousing. My cock is already at attention simply from putting my lips on her skin.

I follow her lead, listening to her small sounds of satisfaction for cues on where to focus my efforts. She's extra sensitive on her hip bones, and if I lick and nip circles there while playing with her breasts, she starts to shudder. Every touch is a lesson in her body, and in what brings her pleasure. It's a lesson I plan on acing over and over again.

"Please, I need more," she moans, and I lift myself up her body to kiss her lips in response.

"Anything. Everything. It's yours."

I make my way down her body again, settling between her legs. To ward off the early morning chill, I lift the blankets over me to cover her, cocooning myself in the darkness. Her scent is even more powerful now, captured by the blanket, and it's the ultimate aphrodisiac for me. I dive into her folds with my tongue, lapping up and down the length of her sex with long, slow licks. I hear her gasp out my name, and her legs bend so her feet are planted on either side of my head. My hands go to her hips, holding her to my face as I devour her. I could die a happy man right now in this moment, knowing it's me making her feel this good. And when she starts to convulse, her hips lifting to meet my mouth, I don't back down. I suck and nip, lick and swirl my tongue around her stiff clit, until she's screaming my name over and over.

One thing I know for certain is this: my body and soul were made for pleasuring her.

Outside the bakery later in the morning, she pulls me in for a hug. My arms fit around her, and I want nothing more than to just hold her there forever.

"Thank you for last night," she says softly, lifting up on her toes so our lips meet.

"I only want to make you happy." I bring my hands to the back of her head, cradling it gently as I kiss her again.

With a groan she steps back and shakes her head at me. "You're making it really hard for me to go and teach yoga," she teases.

"Then my plan is working." I wink. She rolls her eyes, and goes up the stairs to her apartment with a laugh. "Bye, Ethan. I'll see you later," she calls down from the top of the stairs.

"See you soon, shorty." I turn to go to my office, a huge grin on my face. It's been a long time since I felt this happy. And it's all thanks to her.

But my good mood fades away quickly when I power up my computer, and see the email waiting for me. It's from a huge hotel developer, Devereaux Hotels International. I skim the email, then read it again to make sure I understand. Apparently, it's a courtesy notification to me as mayor, informing me that they plan on making an offer to the new owner of Oceanside Resort. I assume somebody at Devereaux heard that the land title was changing hands, and this would be a good time to try and make an offer to the new owner. It makes sense; oceanfront property is at a premium. And one of their luxury hotels would work well on that piece of land.

The thing is, Summer is the new owner of Oceanside resort. Which means they want to offer to buy it from her. Logically I know that she's happy here, and that the chance of her leaving Dogwood Cove, even if she did sell, is small. But the fear remains. What if I'm not enough to keep her here?

Over a week has passed since the work party, and I still haven't told her about the email from Devereaux Hotels. She's spent every night at my house, we've cooked dinner together, we've gone for runs together, she's tried to teach me yoga, and we've fallen into bed and into each other's arms night after night. And I haven't told her that someone wants to buy the resort from her. Even knowing how stressed she is about finding money for the renovations, I just can't bring myself to tell her, even as the guilt eats me alive. Instead, I've been desperately trying to come up with another solution to her money problems, a solution that doesn't involve selling the resort.

I'm plating up some eggs and toast for breakfast when she comes downstairs with a bag full of clothes. The sight makes me frown.

"You really should just leave more stuff here, or heck, leave all your stuff here. Then you wouldn't have to go back to the apartment to change all the time."

"What?" she says, sounding surprised by my suggestion. I put down the pan of eggs and look over at her. I can't deny I'm disappointed by the uncertainty on her face. A seed of doubt gets planted in my mind. Does she not feel the same way I do about us and our future?

"Just an idea, that's all." I go back to cooking breakfast and she doesn't say anything else. We eat quickly, and there's a weird tension in the air that wasn't there before. Later, we walk to the bakery together. I'm meeting Finn to show him around, and she's planning on spending the day at the resort, painting. Turner gifted her all the paint she is going to need for the interior and exterior of the cabins and the main lodge. He tried to say it would have gone to waste anyway, since it was all rejects and mismatched colours, but I saw the shine in his eyes when he gave it to her. Logically I know that she's happy here, and the chance of her leaving Dogwood Cove, even if she did sell, is small. But the fear remains. What if I'm not enough to keep her here?

After she goes upstairs to get ready for her day, I sit at one of the stools that lines the counter along a wall of the bakery, and reread the email that is haunting me while I wait for Finn to arrive. He's coming into town today to check everything out and look for a place to live. If he's the same as he was in university, the guy runs at least ten minutes late for everything.

"What's got you stressed, big brother?" Mila wanders over and sits down beside me.

I don't want to tell her about Devereaux Hotels and their interest in the resort. She'll want to tell Summer; I know she will. But at the same time, I need to talk to someone, and she has always been my go-to person. Even Reid and I don't talk about as many things as Mila and I do. Losing our parents bonded us in a way nothing else can. She knows my secrets and I know hers.

"Let's just say that thanks to being Mayor, I know something I wish I didn't. And I should tell someone, but I don't want to." I'm purposefully vague, hoping Mila can't read between the lines. But I clearly underestimate the power of her intuition.

"Does this have to do with Summer?" she asks, taking a large bite of a muffin, her gaze never wavering from mine.

Seriously, Mila could have a job as a fucking mind reader for how close she is to the truth. And she must see something in my face that makes me look guilty, because she frowns and puts her muffin down.

"Ethan. She's like family. You cannot keep secrets from her."

"I know I can't. But this, it's complicated." I run my fingers through my hair in frustration.

"You guys are dating. You can't keep secrets from someone you're dating! What the heck is so bad that you can't tell her?" Mila says, dropping her voice low.

Before I can overthink my decision, the truth pours out of me. "Devereaux Hotels International want to buy Oceanside Resort from her. They sent me an email, expressing their intention to contact the new owner of the resort about purchasing the land and developing it."

"Ethan you *have* to tell her." Mila says, her voice rising again. "She'll find out eventually; property ownership is public record. They can look it up any time now that the land title has changed to her name."

I put my coffee down with a sigh. "I know, Mills. But what good does it do me to tell her now? She'll know I've kept it from her."

"So, what? You never tell her and hope she doesn't find out that you knew before she did? Life doesn't work that way, Ethan. You've got to come clean, apologize for not saying anything sooner, and hope she forgives you for lying by omission."

I nod slowly. She's right; I know she's right. And I know how Summer feels about lying. I've really dug myself in deep.

My little sister gives a small smile, then lightly slaps me on the shoulder. "Come clean with her. You're not good at keeping secrets."

Just then the door opens and Finn walks in. My sister's ear-piercing shriek leaves no question as to her reaction at seeing Finn again.

"Finn McNeill! Get your scrawny ass over here and give me a hug!"

I groan at my sister's greeting. "Seriously, Mills? I don't need to hear you talk about his ass ever again."

"You're just jealous." Finn winks at me over Mila's shoulder.

These two tried to date once, during the year we all happened to be in Vancouver for university at the same time. It didn't work out, but they did manage to stay friends. Friends who love to give me shit about their past. Despite that, the idea of Finn moving to town makes me really happy.

"Alright you two, break it up. Mila, don't you have cookies to decorate or something?"

Mila rolls her eyes at me. "Oh, relax big brother." Turning back to Finn, she rests her hand on his arm. I narrow a glare at them, but Finn just smirks at me. He knows this riles me up, the fucker.

"Can I get you a coffee? Muffin? Croissant?"

"Thanks, Mila, but I'm good. Maybe after your brother shows me around town we can stop here for lunch. Do you still make that multigrain sourdough bread?"

I cross my arms in front of my chest, watching them be all chummy with each other. "If you're done chatting about baked goods, can we get going?"

Mila walks over and smacks my shoulder. "Calm-. Down. I'm allowed to catch up with an old friend."

Finn chuckles and comes to join us. "Okay, let's go, big man. Show me this amazing town of yours."

We walk out the door of the bakery, only to be stopped by Hattie Henderson. "Mayor Monroe, I was going to come by city hall to have a conversation with you about our Summer. I was hoping to get your advice on how to approach something with her."

Cryptic, but sort of in line with what we expect from Hattie. She's kindhearted but takes the word *eccentric* to a new level at times.

"Sure, Mrs. Henderson. Just call the front desk and have them put you on my calendar during one of my office days."

Hattie nods satisfied with my response and carries on into The Nutty Muffin.

"*Our* Summer?" Finn says, one eyebrow raised at me. I shove him, and not gently.

"Shut up."

"She's the girl from the market, right? Sounds like it might be getting serious."

I nod. "It is."

"But?"

Damn. I forgot Finn is almost as intuitive as my sister. That's probably part of why they never worked out as a couple.

"But I need to tell her something, and it might change how serious things are."

"The Ethan I know never held back from doing what had to be done."

We've reached the gazebo, and I lean against the railing, looking around the town square and thinking of the last time I was here, with Summer.

"The Ethan you know never had so much to lose," I answer bluntly.

"Fuck," he swears under his breath. "That bad?"

"Yeah."

Thankfully, Finn doesn't push for any more details. We stand there in silence for a few minutes before I push off the railing and turn toward the street that leads to the residential neighborhoods.

"Come on. You wanted to see some of the houses we've got available for rent, right?"

He watches me for a minute, and I meet his gaze steadily. After a second he nods, and we set off. We take our time walking up and down the streets as I fill Finn in on life in Dogwood Cove. He's not as into the outdoors as I am and straight up laughs when I mention surfing on the coast.

"Dude, that water is fucking frigid. I wouldn't surf in California, I'm sure as shit not going to surf up here."

"What do you think wet suits are for? If you're going to live here, you need to embrace the elements, man. If you won't try surfing, how about mountain biking? Skiing? Kayaking?" I rattle off several other popular activities, trying to contain my laughter as Finn shakes his head at every one.

"I'll stick to running, on pavement, and hitting the gym when I need to."

"Man, California turned you into a pansy," I can't resist teasing.

"Really? What are you benching these days?" Finn fires back.

"One ninety on a good day," I reply, and he grins triumphantly.

"Two hundred, bitch. Which means you can take your freezing water and death mountains and suck it."

Well, damn. Finn's hiding some muscles under that slick exterior. I have to give him that point, but I'm still not going to let him get away with being such a city boy. Not if he really wants to move here.

"Death mountains is a little extreme, don't you think?"

He shakes his head vehemently. "No way. I watched the episode of Alone where they got lost up on the north end of the island. That's not gonna be me."

I bark out a laugh at that. "You're fucking kidding me, right? That show is total bullshit. They were ten minutes from a Tim Hortons the entire time. Have you ever been up there? It's not the Rocky Mountains, it's Vancouver Island. Pretty hard to get lost for very long."

Finn glares at me. "You're not selling me on this shit, Ethan. I took the job with Pierre for the challenge of starting something new with a legend like him. You living in the area was a bonus. But don't think for one second you're gonna get me doing any of that nature crap."

I hold up my hands in defeat. "Fine. I guess I'll show you the local gym next, then."

An hour later and Finn's convinced. The winery he and Pierre are opening will be located just twenty minutes outside of town. We found him a house he's interested in and he's already left a message for the landlord. He even checked out the gym and the track at the high school and deemed them adequate for his fitness needs. Yeah, you best believe I rolled my eyes at that. Instead of going back to Mila, I manage to convince him to go somewhere else to eat, so we stop in at the pub for lunch. Over a pint of local beer and a burger, we continue to catch up.

"After the third bachelorette party of the day you get pretty tired of the drunk bridesmaids who just *have* to meet the man who makes their 'favourite wine, like, ever.'" Finn huffs out a sarcastic laugh. "Honestly, that's part of the appeal of coming here. A smaller market, sure, but also that it's not the tourist trap Napa's become."

I detect a note of fatigue in his voice. Something that tells me all those years in California weren't sunshine and roses.

Later that afternoon, once I drop Finn back at his car outside the bakery, I make my way over to the grocery store to grab a few things. As I'm walking up and down the aisles, wondering if Summer would be interested in a picnic tomorrow, my phone vibrates with a text message.

SUMMER: Hey, would you mind if I spent tonight at my place?

What the hell? My stomach plummets. I knew she wasn't okay this morning. Did I push too hard by asking her to leave clothes at my place? Shit. I tamp down my panic enough to type out a reasonable reply.

ETHAN: I'll miss you, but if you need some time at home, of course that's fine with me.

SUMMER: Thanks, I've just got a lot I need to

figure out with the resort, and I'm really tired. Someone... likes to keep me up *winky face emoji* *heart emoji*

Okay, the playful tone of that message makes me feel better. But I'm still worried I pushed her too fast. Before I can type out anything else, another message comes through, this one letting me release some of the tension that creeped into my shoulders with her messages.

SUMMER: And I was thinking, I need a day off from paint fumes and hauling trash. Want to hike to the hot springs tomorrow?

ETHAN: Sounds awesome. I'll pick you up in the morning.

Obviously, things aren't so bad between us if she wants to see me tomorrow. And maybe I can somehow get her to see I didn't mean to pressure her with my offer about leaving stuff at my house. As for the hot springs, that's easy. Do I want to see Summer in a bikini? That's a no brainer. Will it give me an opportunity to tell her about Devereaux? Also, yes. But will I take that opportunity? Fuck if I know.

Chapter 19

Summer

Ethan and I are not spending the night together for the first time since our do-over date at his house. His suggestion this morning that I leave more clothes at his house threw me for a minute. We aren't ready to live together, to take that next step. I care about him, but so much in my life is changing right now. I need to take a step back and figure a few things out by myself. For ten years I've been independent, relying on no one but myself. But since coming back to Dogwood Cove, I've realized that being independent and alone is not as good as being supported and loved. Now I need to find the happy balance where I take care of myself, but stay open to the help everyone wants to offer.

When I get home after teaching my yoga class, I sit on the floor of my apartment with a notebook and a glass of wine and try to organize myself. Looking around the small, furnished studio, I write down the word *rent* in big letters. I can't freeload off of Mila and Ethan forever, and we still haven't discussed how much the rent for this place would be. I've always lived quite frugally, so my other expenses don't amount to much. My goal is to dedicate the majority of any income I have to the resort. Yesterday while Ethan showed Finn around, I stopped by the bank and was able to open a small business account and negotiate a deal in fees. That was step one to ensuring that the resort is truly my future. Step two is figuring out exactly what I need to reopen; the bare minimum at first, so I can get operational. For the next several minutes I write furiously, my mind whirring with everything that I think I'll need.

"Holy crap on a cracker," I mutter when I realize how long that list is. It's not just the repairs, or the supplies for the repairs, there is also furnishings, décor, business setup stuff like computers and software, equipment for activities, staffing...the list keeps growing. As does my realization that I don't have a freaking clue what I'm doing. I might have taken some night classes in business management, but nothing that could have prepared me for an undertaking this big. This is starting to feel like the makings of a complete and utter disaster of monumental proportions.

"What the hell were you thinking, Dad?" I ask out loud, wishing he could actually answer me. Maybe he had some grand plan as to how this would all work. Not that it would help me now, since no one has come forward with the answer to all my problems. Needless to say, Dad doesn't answer me. I'm alone here, in a tiny apartment over a bakery, in a town I haven't been lived in for almost two decades.

Not alone. I have Ethan.

I do. And Mila, Serena, Paige. Heck Mrs. Henderson, Reid, Pete and Turner would probably help me again if I needed it. I'm not alone. Not anymore. And maybe this was Dad's plan. Get me back to Dogwood Cove and show me that even with all the years between us, I still have a home and people who care about me. And with their love and support, I'm finding myself and the path I'm meant to be on.

My phone rings, and looking at the screen to see that Mom is calling me stirs up some very mixed feelings. I'm so angry at her, but also hurt and confused. I don't expect answers, at least not any that I can trust, so I hit ignore on her call. I don't have the mental energy to spare on her right now.

I stand up and wander into the tiny kitchen area to refill my wine. Now that I have the list of what I need, it's time to figure out how to get it. Maybe I can barter with Turner for some of the less expensive supplies. His wife was one of the students at my yoga class; if Serena is willing, maybe I can work out a trade. But that only covers a tiny portion of my list. What I really need is money, and lots of it. Too bad my dad didn't also leave a fat bank account along with the run-down resort. But from what Mrs. Henderson was saying, he spent all his savings on the purchase of the property, then fell sick before he could do anything about the renovations. I won't qualify for any type of loan, not with my nonexistent credit history, so my only options are to win the lottery or suck it up and figure out a way to pay for everything myself.

It's only when my second glass of wine is empty, and I'm no closer to solving my problems, that I realize I wish Ethan was here. After all, they do say orgasms are natural stress relievers. I briefly consider texting him, but it's close to midnight. So, I brush my teeth and crawl into bed alone, hoping that my dreams hold the answers I need. I'm now certain it was Ethan in that dream with me and my dad back before the letter came from the lawyer.

I dreamt of Mrs. Henderson.

What the hell that means, I don't know. Especially since she was wearing a gigantic green hat and kept telling me to mind the gap. Either my subconscious wants to be in London, or the wine affected me more than I thought it did.

When I get out of bed the next morning, I have half an hour before I am meant to meet Ethan at the bakery. I spend twenty minutes of that time in the shower, both trying to wake up and clear my mind. Before I fell asleep, I resolved to treat today like a mini vacation from everything that is worrying me right now. Just enjoy a day with Ethan, exploring the beauty of the west coast. Even as a child I never went to the hot springs, but I heard about them. I know there are a few pools there that are big enough for only two people, private and surrounded by nothing but trees.

I dress in my bikini, then pull on some workout leggings and a T-shirt over top. A sweater, a towel, and a water bottle go into my backpack, then I grab my keys and go downstairs. When I push open the door to the bakery, it's already bustling with the morning crowd. Mila and her staff are hurrying around, taking orders, pouring drinks, and serving pastries. She sees me and waves. I wave back before slowly making my way to the side of the front counter. I'm watching the door for Ethan when the sensation of hands snaking around my waist makes me jump.

"Relax, shorty, it's just me," Ethan's warm chuckle fills my ear. I pivot and throw my arms around his neck, pulling him in for a kiss.

"I missed you last night," I whisper.

"Me too. Let's not do that again."

I nod, feeling a smile creep over my face. "Deal. Sorry."

Ethan pulls back, frowning slightly. "Don't apologize. You needed a bit of space, that's fine. As long as that's all you needed."

"It was," I answer quickly, kissing him again. He takes it deeper this time, slanting his mouth over mine, his tongue darting in between my lips, opening me to him.

"Hey lovebirds, break it up. I'm trying to run a respectable establishment here." Mila's teasing cuts in between us.

Ethan pushes her away without breaking contact with my lips, but my giggle forces me back.

"Sorry, Mila."

She hands us a paper bag, then shoos us away. "Go. Leave for your romantic day in nature while the rest of us slave away at work."

Ethan leads me out of the café, with a backwards wave to Mila. We walk to his truck, where he holds the door open for me, then leans in for a chaste kiss once I'm in.

"I'm excited for today."

I smile. "Same."

On the drive to the hot springs trail, I tell Ethan about what I figured out last night. About how I'm fully committed to reopening the resort and seeing my Dad's plan through to completion, no matter how long it takes. He's silent through it all, holding my hand and staring straight out the front windshield. It's not exactly the reaction I thought I would get; I figured he would be more encouraging about my idea to barter for supplies and slow down my timeline for reopening. When I bring up the idea of paying rent on the apartment, he scoffs, and his grip tightens around the steering wheel.

"You don't need to pay us, Summer."

My mouth drops open. "Yes, I do. I'm not going to mooch free rent from you guys forever."

Finally, he spares a glance over at me. His jaw is set in a determined line. "It's not like it costs us anything to let you stay for free for a while longer."

"Ethan. I can't."

Suddenly he turns the steering wheel sharply and pulls to the side of the road. When the truck is stopped, he turns in his seat to face me.

"Summer, listen. There's not a lot I can do for you when it comes to the resort. I can help, and give you my time, but I don't even have much of that to spare. The one thing I, and Mila, can and want to do, is let you stay in the apartment for free. We've talked about it, and we both feel the same way. This is what we can do for you, so please let us."

I'm wondering how the hell I got so lucky, and how on earth I can ever pay them back, when he continues, tapping his chin with a teasing grin.

"But, if you really want to pay rent, I accept orgasms as payment. Yours or mine."

That makes me laugh instead of cry, and I unbuckle my seatbelt so I can shift close enough to kiss him. He takes it further, pulling me into his lap. Even with the steering wheel digging into my back, I feel myself relaxing into his touch. But when I go to reach for the waistband of his shorts, he covers my hand with his.

"Nuh uh. We're going on this hike." His eyes are alight with desire, but his words are full of teasing.

With an exaggerated huff, I move back to my seat. Somehow, he manages to lightly smack my ass on the way.

"Don't worry, there will be time for you to start paying me once we're at the springs."

We get back on the road, and within a couple of minutes we're at the trailhead for the hot springs. There are no other cars in the parking lot, and I shiver with anticipation at the thought of having the entire place to ourselves, no one to hear us or see us.

Ethan grabs our packs and helps me get mine on and fitting comfortably before we set out on the trail.

"We'll have to watch for bears," he says casually, patting a yellow canister at his side. "But I've got bear spray. Just stay close to me, I'll keep you safe."

"My plaid-covered hero," I tease, nudging his arm, which is, in fact, covered in yet another plaid shirt.

"Hey, you like my plaid."

"Mmm hmm, I do. Doesn't mean I'm not going to tease you about being a lumberjack."

He raises his eyebrow at me. "I've got a big axe and I'm not afraid to use it."

"Oh my God." I dissolve into giggles. "That was beyond cheesy."

Ethan tugs me along the path, and I stumble after him, still trying to contain my laughter. But soon the beauty of the nature surrounding us stuns me into silence, and we walk quietly, enjoying nothing more than the sound of birds chirping, and the trees rustling in the light breeze. It's a perfect spring day, the kind that makes you hopeful for new beginnings and such.

Eventually we arrive at the hot spring pools. The first one is quite large and is evidently the most popular one. It has natural benches carved into the stone, and a shallow entry point. But we don't stop there. Ethan carries on up the trail, before turning off the path and leading me between some trees.

Out of nowhere, heaven appears — if heaven is a small pool with hot water burbling out of it, lush trees, and moss-covered rocks everywhere, along with sunlight dappling down through the trees.

"Oh, Ethan, it's perfect," I say quietly, not wanting to disturb the peace. When I turn back to him, he's taking off his shirt. My eyes watch appreciatively as his muscles ripple in front of me. He catches me watching and he grins before sauntering over to me, and slowly lifting my shirt off. When my bikini is revealed, he rumbles an incoherent sound as his gaze roves over my body. The tiny red triangles don't cover much, and I can sense how much he enjoys the sight emanating from his body in waves.

Hand in hand we slowly lower ourselves into the warm water. It's the perfect temperature; not quite as warm as a hot tub, but warmer than bath water. The contrast between the cool spring air and the warm water is delicious and instantly hardens my nipples.

"Come here," Ethan says, only it comes out as a growling command, one I cannot help but obey.

I move over to straddle his lap.

"I'm dying to get inside of you, but I won't. Not here, where anyone could see. Your pleasure is for me, and me alone."

God, this filthy alpha side of him is hot. I squirm in his lap. Surely he doesn't mean we aren't going to do anything?

"There's no one else here right now," I say, the words coming out on a moan as I rub myself along the rigid outline of his cock.

"Fuck," he rasps, then his hands go to my bikini bottom, and his fingers slide underneath to find my sex. "Slippery. You're desperate, aren't you?"

"Yes," I gasp. "Please."

He bends down and kisses my neck, then bites softly before licking away the pain. "I've got you."

I try valiantly to get my hand around him, but our hips are too close together and his hand is in the way. Then my mind blanks when his finger curls around and rubs my inner wall in the exact place I need him. My head falls back, and he kisses the hollow of my neck. Over the roaring in my ears, I can hear him saying something, but I'm too caught up in the orgasm that is hurtling toward me. I've never come this fast in my life, but it must be only mere seconds before I'm screaming out his name into the wilderness.

Afterward, we sit in the water wrapped up in each other's arms. It's the perfect respite from everything that's happened in the last few weeks. I want to come back, maybe in the winter when snow is falling. We talk about nothing important, playing twenty questions to learn the mundane things about each other that we don't already know. Favourite TV shows, sports teams, colours, that sort of thing. I never want to leave, but when we hear voices coming closer through the trees, I know our time alone in this idyllic place has come to an end.

The hike back to the truck seems to go by much faster, and soon we're driving back to town. When we get to the road that would take us to the main drag where my apartment is, Ethan looks at me, asking a silent question.

"Take me to your place, Ethan."

There's no way I want to be apart from him again.

Chapter 20

Ethan

Waking up with Summer in my arms every morning is like nothing else in the world. For a few moments before the pressures of the day hit, I can simply enjoy the feel of her warm body tucked against mine. Something shifted between us at the hot springs. I know my emotions for her are growing stronger; hell, I almost told her I loved her while we were in that warm water. But the timing wasn't right. At the time I didn't know why, but now I do. It's not right because I'm still not being honest with her. In the week since we went for our hike, we have spent every night together, and every opportunity I've had to tell her about Devereaux Hotels, I've choked.

At this point, I know I'm a goddamn idiot. If I had come clean right from the start, it would be a nonexistent issue. And as Mila said, there is nothing stopping the company from reaching out to Summer directly. I can see now that it's really not that big of a deal if she does decide to sell, not that I think she would. Summer's home now, and she is settled into Dogwood Cove as if she never left.

The stress of keeping it from her is starting to show. We might be closer than ever while in bed, when the lights are off and there is nothing between us, but during the day it's different. Whether I'm helping her at the resort, or working in the office, I know she can tell something's wrong. She might think I don't see her worried glances, or the hesitation before she kisses me sometimes, but I do. It kills me, knowing I'm the one responsible for her anxiety.

We've settled into what should feel like bliss-filled domesticity, but instead, my head is ruining it for me by constantly reminding me of how much I'm risking every moment that passes with this hanging over me.

When she kisses me goodbye at the door this morning, I can't shake the sense of foreboding. I know things are going to break, I just don't know when, or how it'll turn out after.

"When I get home tonight, we need to talk," Summer says gently, her hand on my chest. I drop my head to meet hers, covering her hand in mine. "Something's wrong, Ethan, and you need to tell me what it is so I can help."

God, this woman. Her heart is pure gold. But she won't want to help when she finds out why I'm struggling. "I'm falling for you, Summer Harris," I whisper to her, trying to hide the desperation I'm feeling. "No matter what, I'm so glad you came home." I want so badly to tell her I love her. Because fuck, I do. But that would be cruel — to tell her that and then tell her I haven't been completely honest with her.

But there's no mistaking that it's love shining on her face when she smiles at me. "I'm glad I came home, too. And I've already fallen for you, Ethan Monroe." She presses one more kiss to my lips, and then she's gone.

I spend the entire five minute drive to city hall going back and forth over how to deal with things. Maybe I can reach out to Devereaux and try to get him to let it go. Convince him he doesn't want the resort. It would be a huge overstepping of boundaries, seeing as technically I have nothing to do with the resort, and legally I can't exactly stop Devereaux from reaching out to Summer, but it's starting to feel like my only option. Except that would mean I'd be lying to Summer for as long as we're together. Which I want to be forever.

I can't lie to her for the rest of our lives. It's not who I am, and I know it's not the man she would want to be with.

"Fuck," I curse to myself under my breath. There is nothing but problems with no solutions facing me, and I don't know what to do. I've never been in this situation before, and I hate it.

I walk down the hall to my office with only a minimum acknowledgement to the front desk staff. City hall is surprisingly busy, and it takes me a minute before I remember why. Planning for the Summer Solstice festival is underway. It's an annual tradition in Dogwood Cove and something I was really looking forward to attending with Summer by my side.

When I enter my office and turn my ancient computer on, I take a minute to review the messages left for me in the few days since I was here. There are a few meeting requests and note from one of the receptionists stating Mrs. Henderson is coming in for a meeting today. But it's the email sitting at the top of my inbox that makes my hands curl into fists.

Mayor Monroe,

I am extending this email to you personally, as a courtesy. I will be coming to Dogwood Cove to speak with the owner of Oceanside Resort this week. My team and I are moving ahead with our plan to purchase the resort and construct a hotel that will provide a luxury experience for all visitors to the area.

Perhaps we can connect when I am in town. I recognize the value of having a town official such as yourself on my side when it comes to permit applications and hope to further build our working relationship.

Regards,

Cole Devereaux

CEO Devereaux Hotels International

Shit. Fucking shit. Goddamn. He's coming here. If he shows up in town and finds Summer before I've had the chance to come clean, I know even my worst-case scenario won't begin to cover how upset she'll be.

I pick up the phone and dial the number for his Vancouver office, but his receptionist tells me he's not in the office today. Fuck. Opening a new email message, I try to craft a suitable reply.

Mr. Devereaux,

My apologies for my late reply, you are correct that my responsibilities have kept me from answering you until now. I regret to inform you that the owner of Oceanside

Resort will not be interested in selling. I would hate for you to come all this way for nothing.

Regards,
Ethan Monroe
Mayor of Dogwood Cove

It's short and to the point, and I click send before I can second-guess my actions, or the outright lie I just told him. After all, I have absolutely no authority to tell him that Summer doesn't want to sell. Then I sit and stare at the computer screen, willing a response to come through. Surely a business mogul such as Cole Devereaux is checking his emails constantly, right? But five minutes pass with nothing, then ten. One of the receptionists sticks her head in the door to remind me of the meeting for which I'm running late. I nod at her distractedly, still watching my screen. Nothing.

Shit. Okay. *Try not to panic, Ethan.* He said he was coming this week. Maybe he's in a meeting and can't respond right away. Check again after awhile. I give myself a pep talk as I stand and walk to the meeting room for the festival planning session, resigning myself to an hour of nodding politely while the committee work out whatever it is they want to do this year.

But when I get back to my office, there still is no reply. A knock at my door has me looking up to see Hattie Henderson walking into the room. "Mayor Monroe, I have an appointment with you," she says by way of greeting.

"Mrs. Henderson. Please, sit down," I gesture to the chairs in front of my desk, taking one for myself so that we can face each other. This is the last thing I want to be doing right now with the spectre of Cole Devereaux hanging over me, but I have no choice. "What can I do for you?"

The older lady folds her hands in her lap after adjusting the purple hat she's wearing. Hattie and her hats. It's something that makes everyone in town smile when they see her, because she seems to have an endless supply of different hats. I honestly don't know if I've ever seen her wear the same one twice.

"May I call you Ethan for this conversation? It really is more about you as a man than you as a mayor," she says, and I'm a bit taken aback by her candid tone.

"Of course you may."

"Wonderful. Now, Ethan. As I mentioned the other day outside of your sister's bakery, this is about our Summer. You know I was close to her father, and to her when she was a young child. Well, there's more that I haven't told anyone yet, including Summer, and my hope is that you can help me find an appropriate way to discuss it with her."

I nod slowly, even as my mind is screaming at me to run in the other direction. The last thing I need is more secrets to keep from Summer.

"Carl informed me of his plan to purchase Oceanside Resort long before he actually did so. He wanted an honest opinion on his plan, and I was happy to give it to him. When he retired from the postal service, he had a tidy retirement plan, but it wouldn't have been enough to purchase Oceanside outright and pay for the renovations, which was his goal." She frowns, looking down at her hands before bringing her gaze back to mine. I'm shocked to see her eyes are wet with tears. "Carl would have been devastated if he knew what a mess Summer had to face when she returned. He wanted to have the place all fixed up and ready to go before she came home. I saw him, you know, the day he died. He held my hand and made me promise I would see our deal through."

"Your deal?" I interrupt, sitting up straighter. This is the first I'm hearing of any sort of agreement or deal about Oceanside. My heart starts to thump faster. Could there actually be an answer to Summer's struggles?

"Yes, our deal. We kept it very quiet; Carl didn't want to advertise my situation any more than necessary," she replies primly. "My husband was a wealthy man, Ethan. He died before I moved here, and he left me with more money than any one person should need. I was at a loss as to what to do with it all, having no family of my own, until Carl and sweet Summer came into my life. Then, before I knew it, they became my family. When Carl approached me with his idea of opening Oceanside, I saw it as a chance for me to give back to him for all the companionship he'd given me over the years." She sniffs delicately, withdrawing a handkerchief from her purse and dabbing at her eyes. "It's lonely living by yourself. Carl would visit me often, help around the house, fetch me groceries, and we would talk about Summer all the time. How much we both missed her. I saw her as my kin, my granddaughter, from all those times I would babysit her. And now I want to help her the same way I was going to help Carl."

I try to conceal my astonishment when Hattie Henderson reaches into her purse and draws out a cheque.

She passes it over to me, and when I see the amount written there, my jaw drops.

"Mrs. Henderson, this cheque is for a hundred thousand dollars," I stammer out.

"Yes, dear. That's the amount I was going to give Carl, to be a silent investor, if you will, in the reopening of Oceanside Resort. Now that money is Summer's."

I'm dumbfounded. Shocked into silence. My mind is going a mile a minute, but I can't formulate any words or even a response. I give the cheque back to her, noticing my hands are shaking.

"I'll give it to her when she comes for tea tomorrow. I trust you can keep this to yourself until then?"

"Yes. Of course," I gulp audibly. Only one day. I can manage one day of holding another secret from Summer. Hell, maybe I won't tell her about Devereaux until after she talks to Hattie. Maybe that will ease the blow.

I walk Mrs. Henderson to the door and say goodbye before going back to my chair and sinking down into it. But before I can regroup at all, my office door flies open again. This time, it's my sister. But she isn't alone.

"What the fuck is that, Mills?" I shoot back up to standing, and stare down at the giant dog at her side. A length of rope has been lightly looped around his neck, and my sister is holding the other end.

"A dog, idiot. I need you to figure out our animal control situation. This guy was wandering the highway. No tags, no collar, nothing. He's obviously tame, so who the hell dumped him? If we had animal control, we could take care of him. Instead, I have to."

I arch my brow. "*You have to*? Or you want to."

Mila huffs at me. "I'm not going to leave him abandoned to the elements, Ethan. And we don't even have an animal shelter nearby. So, what, I drive him to Victoria? That's pointless."

I wave at her dismissively as I sit down again and open a new email that has just come through. "Okay, whatever, Mills. *Shit.* I need to find Summer."

I reread the message again to make sure I am understanding it properly.

Mayor Monroe,

I am on my way to Dogwood Cove and look forward to meeting with you after my conversation with the owner of Oceanside Resort.

Regards,

Cole Devereaux

CEO of Devereaux Hotels International

I've forgotten all about my sister and the dog she apparently now owns, until her voice pierces my panic. I jerk my head up to see her narrow her eyes at me accusingly. "Why do you sound freaked out, Ethan?"

"Because Cole Devereaux is on his way here right now to talk to Summer. He's used to getting what he wants, Mila, and he wants the resort. Only she doesn't know that, so she's going to be blindsided by him and his offer."

I stand up abruptly from my desk, making the dog at Mila's feet bark. I frantically grab my jacket, my phone, and my keys before jogging to my office door. Vaguely, I realize Mila and the dog are following me, but my sister doesn't say anything more until we're outside. Then she steps in front of me, blocking my entrance to my truck, her hands on her hips, temper flaring.

"Wait. You're saying you never told Summer about Devereaux? Oh my God, Ethan, you idiot."

"I know I fucked up. Trust me, Mila, no one knows that better than I do. I have to find her and explain, and beg for her forgiveness," I run my fingers through my hair, tugging on the ends roughly. "Fuck. I gotta go. I have to get to her before this guy shows up." I gesture down to the dog as I climb into my truck. "Take the mutt to the vet and get him checked out before you decide to keep him. He could have fleas." Then I peel out of my parking spot and drive to Oceanside Resort, hoping to catch Summer before Cole fucking Devereaux does.

Chapter 21

Summer

Walking into the hardware store fills me with an excitement I never imagined I would feel surrounded by tools and lumber. But coming here to speak with Turner is stage one of my plan. I texted Serena this morning to ask if she was okay with me bartering yoga classes for supplies, and she was on board. Which means I need to approach Turner next and see what he can offer in exchange.

I also need to price out all the windows I'm going to need, so I can figure out how to budget for them. And I need to look for a replacement hammer since I managed to break mine the other day.

Half an hour later, I have a page full of notes about windows, and a new hammer. I head to the front of the store to pay when Turner's cheerful voice reaches me.

"Hey there, Summer, what can I help you find today?"

I turn from the cashier, my hammer and receipt in hand, with a smile for my dad's old friend.

"Hi, Turner. I was hoping to find you. I was wondering how you feel about bartering?"

The look he gives me is curious, but open.

"Let's go to my office and chat."

When I walk out of the store, the sun is shining, and my smile is beaming. With the agreement I've set with Turner, I'll have the windows ready to install within a few weeks. I'm pretty sure he's giving me some sort of discount, but it doesn't feel like a handout. Not with the three months of free yoga classes I've promised his wife in return.

Part one of my plan to take control of my budget issues and my renovation plans was a success. And with Mila and Ethan's generous offer of free rent, all the money from my paycheques from Paige and Serena can go into the resort fund to pay for furnishings and décor. Next weekend will be the perfect time to hit the flea market to see what I can find.

The possibility of success is becoming real to me. More importantly, the possibility of finally having a stable home and a stable future is becoming real.

Like a pin being poked into a balloon to pop it, my phone rings with another call from my mom. I've ignored her twice now, so guilt has me answering.

"Hi, Mom."

"Summer? Well thank god you finally decide to answer. Where are you baby? I haven't heard from you in forever." Maybe it's my new understanding of everything my mom did to me over the years, but she sounds petulant and selfish even with just those few words.

"I'm in Dogwood Cove."

"What the hell are you doing there?" The judgment in her tone instantly raises my defenses. This is my home now, and I won't stand for her criticism. Not now that I know the truth.

"I've moved back home. Did you know Dad died? No, probably not. Because that would mean being aware of someone other than yourself. Well, I'm back, and I'm not leaving. I'm not coming to Niagara, Mom. I'm home."

I hang up the phone, not wanting to hear another word from her mouth. And I'm hit by the realization that I'm not sad about ending my tenuous relationship with my mother.

Not sad at all.

I'm starting to love the drive from Ethan's house to Oceanside Resort. The routine of coming out here every day is so normal and domestic. I would have never guessed that normal was what I was looking for when I came home, but I guess it is. My dad had a good idea when he bought this place, I get that now. Pulling into the parking lot at the resort, I sit in my truck and stare at everything around me for a minute. Compared to when I arrived a little over a month ago, the place is transformed. The pride that infuses me is a new sensation, and a welcome one. I'm pleasantly shocked at how much I've been able to accomplish on my own, along with the help Ethan and our friends have contributed.

The weeds are gone, the grass is cut back, and the ground isn't covered in garbage. The main building and the exterior of all the cabins have been painted, thanks to the donation of paint from Turner. All of the broken windows have been cleaned up, and while many are still boarded, waiting for replacements, there are no longer jagged edges sticking out everywhere. And that's just what I can see from my truck. Climbing down, I wander around the upper field, where I could easily envision some campsites and trailer hook ups. As I walk back down toward the water, I take stock of the property, thinking about what still needs to be done. I'm finally at a stage where I can see the finished resort much more clearly in my head. A swimming dock, floating out in the water. A new patio off the main building with a big grill families can use to cook on. Adirondack style chairs out front of each cabin. I want to make my dad's vision come true of Oceanside Resort being a high quality, comfortable place for families to come and visit.

But daydreaming about the future isn't helping me get there any faster. There's still so much to do, and I know I should get going. Yet, for some reason, today I feel like I deserve to take a few more minutes to simply feel proud of myself. Sitting on the sand, leaning against my favourite log on the beach, I look out at the water and let my eyes fall shut. The sound of the waves, seagulls in the distance, and the feel of the sun on my face are the only things I focus on. As always, I'm grateful to my yoga practice for giving me the ability to just shut out the world and turn my thoughts inward. So many times, I find it's the only path to peace for me. And lately, dealing with finding out Dad died, then Oceanside, then

Ethan...well, it's safe to say peace has been hard to grasp. For good reasons and not so good reasons.

Apparently, the universe has decided that inner peace is not a priority for me right now as the sound of a car driving up pulls me from my reverie. I stand slowly and stretch my arms up high as I smile out at the water. My guess is that it's Ethan, and after I give him crap for being here and not at city hall like he said he needed to be, I might convince him to come down to the beach for some fun. There's a large blanket in the back of my truck that we could spread out, and the log acts as an excellent privacy screen from anyone who might arrive. Although, it's not as if I have many visitors out here.

But when I turn around, it's not Ethan's truck I see parked up by the building. A sleek black sportscar is there instead, and the man climbing out is definitely not my lumberjack. Even from a distance I can tell that this guy was born to wear a suit. Especially when he buttons up the jacket as he looks around, in that casual, hot-guy-wearing-a-suit way.

"Can I help you?" I call out as I walk toward him, keeping a cautious distance. After all, I'm here alone and this man is a total stranger. I pull my phone out and unlock it with my thumb as well. Not that it'll do me much good if he really is here for nefarious reasons, but it makes me feel mildly better.

"Are you Summer Harris?" the suit asks, walking over but stopping at a respectful distance. He gets a point for that.

"Yes, who's asking?"

He seems surprised and somewhat offended by my question. As if I should know who he is. Apparently, his ego is as rich as his car.

"My name is Cole Devereaux, Ms. Harris. I own Devereaux Hotels International. Were you unaware I was coming?"

Holy shit. Cole Devereaux is here, standing in front of me in a suit that probably costs more than my truck. Wait. Why is Cole Devereaux here? I may not have recognized the man standing before me, but even I've heard of Devereaux Hotels. They're a huge company of luxury hotels spread across Canada. So why is their CEO at Oceanside?

"I most definitely was unaware," I say bluntly, my thoughts churning.

"Well then, I apologize for catching you by surprise. That was not my intention, let me assure you. I've actually been trying to reach you for some time," he says smoothly, then his lips thin. "Your town mayor seemed reluctant to provide me with any means to contact you directly." He frowns, clearly unhappy with that.

And I don't blame him, I'm pretty fucking unhappy to hear that as well. Never in a million years would I have guessed Ethan would keep something like this from me. I thought he knew how important honesty was to me.

"What did you want to talk about, Mr. Devereaux?"

"Please, call me Cole." He smiles at me, not bothering to disguise his quick appraisal of my appearance. He may be handsome, but I don't appreciate the attention. Not at all.

"Okay, Cole, then call me Summer." I keep my voice steady and neutral. There's no way I want this snake charmer of a man to know he's rattled me. I'm not scared of him, but I am scared of what I suspect has happened. And that has nothing to do with Cole Devereaux, and everything to do with Ethan Monroe.

He nods. "Excellent, Summer. It's a pleasure to finally make your acquaintance. I wanted to speak with you about an exciting offer I have for you." His eyes roam around the property, and I wonder if he sees what I see. Probably not. He has no idea how bad it was before, and let's be honest, to a man used to luxury the way he obviously is, this place still looks like a dump. "To be frank, I wish to buy this property from you."

My stomach feels heavy and I take an involuntary step back at his words. The voice that has been panicking inside of my brain about my lack of funds is cheering in relief. Sell the property and be done with the stress. But my heart is reminding me of my dad. Of how much he wanted me here, running Oceanside Resort with him. Even with him gone, the idea of not fulfilling his dream hurts. Cole is still talking, but all I hear is a buzzing sound. It's not even the fact that someone wants to buy Oceanside that has me so shocked. No, it's the fact that Ethan obviously knew about this, and didn't tell me. Did Mila know? Serena? Paige? Did everyone but me know there was an option on the table that would eliminate all of my worries? Even if I had no intention of taking it, the very fact that Ethan kept it from me, prevented me from making the decision for myself, hurts deeply. He let me get close to him. I opened up to him physically and emotionally. I thought we were developing something real, something that felt a lot like love, and now I find out he has been, in essence, lying to me for a long time.

"When did you first talk to Mayor Monroe?" I interrupt whatever Cole was saying. Oh God, if he was lying to me even before we crossed the line between friendship and lovers...

"A week or so ago. My team informed him of our intent to contact you about purchasing the land. We've been scouting oceanfront properties on Vancouver Island for some time, and this place has been on our radar for some time."

I nod my head, hearing his words and letting them sink in. Did Ethan know about this the night we spent at the cabin? What about all of the nights since then, when we've fallen asleep together, made love, talked about the future. Did he know? Was he keeping this from me that entire time? My heart is racing, and I feel nauseous. Ethan lied to me.

"Perhaps we could discuss this further over lunch? I really think you'll appreciate the offer I've prepared, and I'd enjoy the opportunity to go over it with you," Cole asks, and though the words are innocent enough, there's an underlying tone that makes me uncomfortable somehow. I realize he's come closer to me.

"I don't think —"

Tires spray gravel everywhere and I look up to see Ethan's truck come to an abrupt stop. Relief and anger do battle in my heart at the sight of him. I don't want to be alone with this Devereaux guy any longer.

He climbs down from his truck slowly, warily, his eyes going from Cole, to me, and then back to Cole, where they narrow slightly.

"Mr. Devereaux, I assume?" he says curtly, striding up to Cole. I watch the two men face off silently, both standing rigid and tall, assessing each other's weaknesses. After several minutes of Ethan looking like he's ready to head into battle, while Cole stands back with a smug expression on his face, I can't stand it anymore.

"Stop fucking staring each other down. What the hell, Ethan, why didn't you tell me about the offer?" I say, breaking their standoff. They turn to me, and the differences in their expressions are stark, almost comical. Ethan is clearly worried about my reaction to everything, while Cole seems triumphant. Which is very presumptuous of the man, seeing as I have given him no indication that I want to take whatever offer he is putting on the table.

"Mayor Monroe, I'm not entirely clear as to why you're here, but you're interrupting our conversation," Cole says in an arrogant tone, not giving Ethan a chance to respond to me. "Summer, let's go into town and sit down over some lunch to discuss things in private. My treat."

"Would you stop hitting on my girlfriend?" Ethan roars as he turns to face Cole. His face is red, and I can see his chest heaving with emotion.

"Oh my God, Ethan, stop!" I cry out. "He's not hitting on me; he's trying to tell me something that *you* should have told me."

My words make Ethan freeze in place. Slowly he turns to me, and his anger at Cole is replaced with remorse and fear.

"I'm so sorry, Summer. I should have, I know that. I don't even know why I didn't," Ethan takes the last few steps until he's right in front of me. I can smell him, his scent calming me, despite my anger at him. "That's not true. I do know. I was scared. So fucking scared that you would take the offer and disappear from my life again. I didn't want to lose you."

"So instead, you decided to lie to me?"

"No, I —"

"You lied to her, Monroe, and to me," Cole interrupts.

"With respect, Mr. Devereaux, you shouldn't be here," Ethan fires back at him, clenching his fists at his side. I put a hand on his shoulder, whether to hold him back or anchor myself, I don't know.

What I do know, with astounding clarity, is that there's nothing Cole Devereaux can offer that would make me sell the resort. Not even my hurt and anger at Ethan lying to me is enough to make me run. This is my home, my resort, and I'm not going anywhere.

"Ethan, stop."

Turning to Cole, I let my hand fall. "I'm very sorry for the miscommunication you experienced, Cole, and I'm equally sorry you came all this way for nothing. I have no interest in selling Oceanside Resort."

"You haven't heard my offer."

"I don't need to. Thank you for your interest, but we're done here."

I stand there, my arms crossed over my chest, staring Cole directly in the eyes. After a moment he nods.

"I understand. I apologize for my part in how this turned out, Summer. And if you ever change your mind, please contact me." He walks over and hands me a business card. When I take it, our fingers brush, and judging by his flirtatious smirk, it was intentional.

I turn away from them both and walk down to the beach. I can hear Ethan's footsteps behind me, and the sound of tires on the gravel tells me Cole is thankfully leaving without anymore of a fight.

Now I only have one presumptuous, arrogant man to deal with, not two.

Chapter 22

Ethan

Fucking Cole Devereaux with his fucking suit and fancy as fuck sportscar. Coming in here and fucking things up.

No, you fucked it up. My conscience pokes at the hole growing in my heart, and it burns like a hot poker. As I follow Summer down to the beach, I'm scrambling on the inside, trying to figure out what to say to make things better. I lied to her. There might not be a way to make that better, but even considering that possibility is making my heart hurt even more.

"Summer, please, can we talk?"

She's come to a stop down at the water's edge, and from the way her arms are wrapped around her midsection, I can tell that touching her right now would be a bad idea. Even still, every part of my body aches to pull her into my arms and hold her until she forgives me.

"I don't know, Ethan, can we talk without you keeping things from me?"

The temperature around us drops several degrees, and not from the weather.

"I'm sorry. I screwed up, and I know it. But please, can you hear me out?" I'm begging, ready to drop to my knees if that's what it takes. But she won't even turn around to look at me. "I know —"

"No, Ethan, you don't get to claim that you know *anything* right now." She finally whirls around, and the tears tracking down her cheeks make me crumble to dust on the inside.

"You *know* how I feel about being lied to. You know how important it is to me that we always tell the truth. When I *fell for you*, I thought I had found a good man. Someone who would be my partner, who I could trust."

She laughs, but it's a hollow sound that will haunt me.

"I guess I was wrong."

"Summer, no. Please don't say that. You can trust me; I am your partner. I made a mistake, a huge one, by not telling you about Devereaux as soon as he reached out to me. Nothing I do or say can take that back, but there has to be something I can do to make you give me another chance. Give *us* another chance."

I risk it and reach out to take her hand, but she pulls back, shaking her head.

"I don't know if I can."

No. No, no, no, no, no. She has to forgive me; this can't be the end. But as she gives me one final, painful glance, then walks slowly back up to her truck, it starts to sink in that maybe this can't be fixed.

"I love you, Summer," I cry out, my voice cracking. I swipe angrily at the wetness on my own cheeks, not wanting tears to blur my vision of her.

She turns around and for a fleeting second, I have a brief flash of hope. Then the anger and pain in her expression hits me with the force of a Mack truck.

"How dare you. How *dare* you say those words now. I can't trust them, Ethan. I can't trust anything you say."

Summer takes off at a run toward her truck and I move to follow but stop myself. I can't, not after what she just said. Instead, I stand there, frozen in my own version of hell, watching the woman I love more than anything on earth drive away from me.

I have no idea how long I stay at Oceanside. All I know is that the light fades, and eventually I am surrounded by the dim, grey light of dusk. It's cold, any trace of springtime warmth gone. The only light comes from a sliver of the moon, and I stumble, tripping over rocks and my own feet as I make my way to my truck. I haven't eaten all day, haven't done anything except sit in misery at my own stupidity. How could I have been so foolish as to think we had a chance of surviving this? A lie of omission is still a lie, and Summer made it clear to me how she felt about trust and honesty thanks to the games her mother played. Not that I can place any blame for this current mess on her mom. Summer has been nothing but open and receptive to me since the beginning. She took a chance on us, before we knew how Mila would feel, before Summer herself even knew what her plans were for the resort. Her feelings for me were strong enough that she trusted I would be there for her no matter what, and I broke that trust completely.

Somehow, I manage to drive back to my house on autopilot. It's a miracle I make it unscathed given how oblivious I feel to anything but my own heartache. *Selfish bastard.* But telling a woman that I love her isn't something I've done before. My sister and my mom not included. Having that love thrown back in my face is a type of pain I have never experienced.

When I get home, traces of her are everywhere, and they hurl themselves at me like tiny daggers. A sweater of hers, draped across the back of a chair. The mug she used for her coffee this morning sitting on the counter beside mine. A heart she drew with our initials in it, taped onto my fridge. Remnants of a broken relationship, a love that could have been, but now may never will be. Like a fool, I go into my bedroom, only it's worse there. It smells of her — sunshine, lavender, peppermint, and happiness. The bathroom has two toothbrushes in the holder, two towels on the rack. Everywhere there are signs of how we were merging our lives together.

My sorrow over losing her mixes with my rage at myself and at Devereaux. Logically, I know that none of this is his fault, but it's so easy to cast blame. If he hadn't wanted the property. If he hadn't come to town. If he hadn't found her before I could tell her the truth.

If I hadn't lied to her.

I make my way into the kitchen, grab the bottle of whiskey and a glass, and go to the couch. Dimly I think about eating something, but the oblivion I can hopefully find with the whiskey is too alluring right now. Anything to dull this pain. Before I can down even one glass, my phone rings. Putting the glass down on the coffee table, I debate not looking at it, ignoring whoever it is. But then I pick it up and see that it's my sister. I don't want to talk to her, yet at the same time some small, sadistic part of me needs to know if she's talked to Summer.

"Hey, Mills."

"What the hell happened, Ethan? I saw Summer parking behind the bakery earlier and run up the stairs to her apartment with tears streaming down her cheeks. She didn't even listen when I called out to her. Is she okay?"

"I...we...shit." My voice breaks on a sob that I can't contain, and I drop my head into my hand.

"I'm coming over."

Ten minutes later, I hear a key in the lock of my front door. I'm on my second glass of whiskey, and slowly starting to feel numb.

"Ethan? Where are you? Why the heck is it so dark in here?"

Mila turns on the lights in my living room, and I blink from the sudden brightness.

"Jesus, Mills. Do you have to turn all the lights on?"

I squint over at the entryway where my sister stands, her hands on her hips. The damn dog is by her side.

"I thought you were taking the dog to the vet?"

"I did. He's healthy, except for some kind of old leg injury, and I'm keeping him for now. But this isn't about the dog. What happened with Summer?"

"Devereaux got to her first."

Mila comes over and sits next to me, and the damn dog jumps onto the couch between us. His head rests on my lap, and it's the first thing all day that almost brings a smile to my face. I lower my hand to his back and stroke his soft coat.

"I hurt her, Mila. She has every right to be angry, to not trust me. But I told her I love her, and she walked away."

"Oh, Ethan."

When I look at my sister, she's shaking her head at me, something akin to pity in her eyes. She reaches for my glass and the bottle of whiskey, eyeing it critically before pouring a measure and drinking it down.

"We need a second glass." She gets up and walks into my kitchen where I hear cupboards opening and closing. She comes back with not only a second glass, but also some crackers and cheese.

"If I'm getting drunk with you, I need food."

On command, my stomach growls.

"I guess you do, too."

I nod silently, taking the cracker and cheese she holds out to me and eat it without tasting anything. I eat another, and another, until Mila finally gives me back my whiskey again.

"What are you going to do?" she asks as she sips her drink. I take a bigger swallow of mine before I answer.

"I have no fucking clue. I could apologize until I'm blue in the face, but she won't believe my words anymore."

"So, don't use words."

The way Mila says it, like earning Summer's forgiveness is so easy, makes me angry. I slam my glass down, making the dog lift his head and woof softly. Pushing his head off my lap I stand and start to pace in front of the coffee table. The inertia I have been fighting for an hour is gone and in its place is an anxious restlessness that I can't avoid.

"Goddamnit, Mills. Don't you think I would do that if I knew how? All I want to do is go to her, grab her and hold on and not let go until she forgives me. I would do anything, *anything* to get her to forgive me. But you didn't hear her. The look on her face when she realized I had lied to her, that's something I'll never be able to forget."

Mila's silent after my outburst. I stare at her desperately, hoping she'll have a solution, or even part of one. Something I can do.

"Do you know why being lied to is such a big deal for her?" Mila asks quietly.

I nod slowly. "Her mom. Not only did her mom lie to her about her dad for so many years, but she also dragged Summer all over the country chasing men and false promises."

"Exactly. She lived for so many years watching men make a fool out of her mother. Saying one thing and doing another. Then she comes home, only to learn that her mother lied to *her* for all those years about her dad. Is it really any surprise that after all that, her trust is easily broken? Hell, I'd say it's a freaking miracle she trusted you at all."

"I know. You're right about all of it. But how do I fix this, Mila?" I make my way back to the couch and sink down. Mila sips her whiskey, looking at the dog who's now draped across her lap.

"Well, first of all, you need to realize that it's not only Summer trusting *you* that's the problem. You need to trust her as well."

"What the hell does that mean?"

"You said that you love her, do you think she loves you?"

I force my mind to clear so I can think about that question seriously. A thousand moments over the last few weeks come back to me.

"Yeah, I do."

"So why didn't you trust that she wouldn't leave if she knew about the Devereaux offer?"

Fuck.

"I...I don't know."

"That's problem number one," Mila states. "Problem number two is, you didn't trust her enough to tell her that you loved her until you were worried about losing her."

"Listen, the last thing I need are more problems. I need solutions," I growl at my sister who is sitting beside me looking smug. "So if you came over to make me feel worse, great, you've succeeded." I down my whiskey, then stand up again and walk to the front window, resting my arm against it, staring out into the darkness.

"Cut the dramatics, big brother, and shut up and listen. I'm here because I happen to love you both." Mila's calm and unruffled, even in the face of my anger. "You need to figure out why you didn't trust your feelings, or her."

"Because she could leave me. And I can't lose someone else that I love," I pivot on my foot to face her and yell the words I didn't even know were inside of me until they came out.

"Holy shit. Is this about Mom and Dad dying?" Mila asks, wide-eyed. "Or Aubrey leaving you?"

Shit. I hadn't even thought about my ex in years, but as soon as Mila says her name, it hits me. She's right. I sink down to the couch. "Both? I don't know."

Mila comes and stands beside me, taking my hand in both of hers and squeezing it tightly.

"Mom and Dad died way too soon, and we're both screwed up from that." There is an angry sadness in Mila's voice that my senses tell me, even dulled by the whiskey, is something to come back to at another time. "And even if you didn't want to admit it at the time, I know that Aubrey leaving so suddenly messed with your head. But that wasn't about you, that was her not being able to handle things like a mature adult. You know that, right?" I nod slowly. "Good. Now that you know *why* you had a hard time trusting your emotions about Summer, you can move on from it. You can accept the fact that you're in love and figure out how to live that truth instead of hiding behind excuses."

"I do love her, Mills. So much."

"I know that. The question is, how are you going to convince *Summer* of that?"

"If I knew the answer, I wouldn't be here getting drunk with you and your dog. No offense."

Mila shifts her body so that she's facing me. "Do you believe she wants to stay in Dogwood Cove, no matter what?"

"Yeah, I do," I admit, realizing it's the truth. Summer has said it enough that I know she's happy here. And as much as I want to say it's because of me, I know it's more than that. She feels like she's home. And she is.

"Okay. Then let's do whatever we can to show her that staying in town is the right choice, and that staying with *you* is even better."

"How?"

"By using actions, not words."

Chapter 23

Summer

When I drive away from the resort, I leave half of my heart behind with Ethan standing on that beach. A battered and bruised half, but half, nonetheless. The entire trip back to town I battle with myself, questioning if I overreacted or not. No. He kept something from me, a really big something. Even if I have no intention of accepting the deal Cole Devereaux wants to offer me, it's my decision to make. Ethan tried to take that choice away from me by hiding this. I just can't understand why he didn't trust me enough to talk to me about it.

The farther away from him I get, the more clearly I can see the real problem. Ethan didn't trust us, or our relationship, enough. And God, does that ever hurt. He claims to love me, but love means trusting someone with your heart. It's more than just pretty words, it's actions, it's the choices we make every day to work together, to be open and honest.

When I reach town, I go straight to the bakery, parking in the back in hopes that Mila won't see me. As I hurry up the stairs to my apartment, I see the back door to the bakery open and hear her call out my name. But I ignore her; there's no way I can face her right now.

Once I'm inside, I sag to the floor, unable to hold myself together any longer. The tears that I fought back the entire drive here pour out of me. I thought I had cried enough at the resort, in front of Ethan. Apparently, I was wrong, there's plenty more to come, and I let them flow. Sadness, anger, frustration, grief, and pain; all the feelings wash over me until I sink into the pile of emotions that overwhelm me.

Eventually my eyes dry. My throat is left raw from crying, and I'm empty inside. *I need to get up.* I stagger into the kitchen where I pour a glass of water, chugging it down greedily. I'm parched. A second glass follows the first before I start to feel the tiniest amount better. Physically, that is. Emotionally I'm still a complete and utter wreck. I turn on my kettle and pull out some herbal tea before going to the fridge for my emergency stash of chocolate. While the water boils, I manage to change into my pajamas, then I take my tea and chocolate and climb under the covers of my bed. In the dim light of my apartment, I take several deep breaths, and close my eyes.

An incessant knocking on my door wakes me from the nap I never intended on taking.

"Summer? Are you in there?"

"Of course she is, Serena, we know she is."

It's Paige and Serena. Crap. Does that mean Mila's with them? She's my best friend, and I know she said all those things about chicks before dicks, but I'm so upset with Ethan I don't know if I can handle seeing her and being reminded of him in any way.

"Summer, please open the door, we need to know you're alright," Paige's voice comes through my door again.

I slowly peel back the covers and drag myself out of bed. My body aches as if I have the flu. But I know it's only my broken heart spreading the pain throughout my body.

Wordlessly, I open the door, then turn and walk back to my bed, picking up my now cold mug of tea and taking it to the kitchen to warm it up. With a sense of relief I note that Mila isn't with them. But Serena has her arms crossed over her chest and is eyeing my outfit critically, while Paige is looking around the apartment.

"This looks much the same as it did when their last renter moved out," she comments.

"I don't have a lot of stuff."

"Have you ever had a place you considered home?"

Paige's question hits me in the heart and I feel my jaw drop slightly.

"Jeez, Paige, way to cut to the chase." Serena shakes her head as she walks over to me and takes my arm, leading me to the couch before pushing me to sit down between them. "What our intelligent friend is getting at is, we want to know if you consider Dogwood Cove your home."

I nod, mutely.

"Okay. Did you ever tell Ethan that?"

Yes, of course I did. Didn't I? I know we spoke about me opening the resort, wanting to see my dad's plan come true. But we didn't have that talk until very recently. I suppose, early on, it may have been unclear what I wanted to do. And my life before here was nomadic at best.

"Here's the thing, Summer," Paige pipes in. "Mila called us as soon as she saw you. She went to talk to Ethan and sent us here."

The jab of hearing his name hurts. And yet, I also desperately want to know how he is. What kind of messed up madness is that.

"He's a wreck, in case you're wondering. He knows he made a big mistake, and is apparently reacting strongly to it."

"That doesn't matter. I know he's sorry, but it doesn't change the fact that he didn't trust me. He lied to me. So how can I ever trust him?" My voice comes out as a croak and I take a sip of my tea, letting the still-warm liquid soothe my throat.

"Did you ever stop to think about why he lied?" Serena takes my hand in hers.

I shake my head dumbly. I still don't have an answer to that question.

"Let's try this from another angle. Did you know Ethan has only been in one serious relationship since their parents died?"

Oh. *Oh.*

"I'm not going anywhere," I blurt out, trying to make sense of this revelation.

"You know that, but does he? Think about it from his perspective, with his past experiences. His mind had him worried that you might have left him if you took the offer from the hotel guy. And you leaving would be another loss of someone Ethan loves. Mila's theory is that her idiot brother couldn't handle that possibility and went about it in a typical man way. By ignoring it."

I stand up, pulling my hand away from Serena. She's making a really good point, but that doesn't mean I want to hear it. Walking over to my bed, I pick up the chocolate bar and take a large bite.

"So, what," I mumble around my mouthful of chocolate. "I'm meant to just forgive him for lying to me, because his parents died, and he's scared I'll leave him like his ex did? That's not fair to me. His problems with trust and honesty screwed this up, not me." The damn tears are threatening to start again, and I swipe at them angrily.

"That's not what we're saying, Summer. You have every right to be mad at him. Hell, I'm pissed at him on your behalf. Remember? Chicks before dicks."

At the sound of Mila's voice, I look up to see her standing in my doorway. Suddenly I forget why I didn't want to see her, because I do. I walk over to her and let her fold me into her arms for a hug.

"I'm sorry, Mila."

"What the hell for?" She holds me at arm's length. "You did nothing wrong. My brother is the idiot who fucked up. That's why I left his drunk ass at his place, with Reid going to check in on him, so that I could come here."

Mila walks us back over to the couch and sits down with me. "He feels awful, Summer. And so do I."

I look at her, confused. "Why do you feel bad? You didn't lie."

She winces. "I sort of did. I knew about the email he received. I told him he had to tell you, and then I just assumed he did. I'm sorry."

I don't have any energy left in me to be upset at her, so I just let my head fall back against the couch.

"You need to get out of town," Mila announces. "Paige, don't you have that book fair thing in Vancouver this weekend?"

My gaze bounces between them, sensing some sort of unspoken conversation that's going on.

"I do. Summer, you should join me," Paige says. The out of the blue offer is suspicious, and I know I'm being manipulated, I just don't know why. But honestly? Getting out of Dogwood Cove for a couple of days sounds amazing.

"When do we leave?"

Traveling to Vancouver with Paige was a really good idea. Some distance from both the town and Ethan is helping me to calm down and process what happened, and Paige is the perfect traveling companion, largely leaving me to my own thoughts. She's a good friend, thoughtful and insightful, but she knows when to back off. I'm grateful for the space I've had to think.

And the time to miss Ethan.

I wish I didn't miss him. I wish I could hold onto my anger, like a protective shield. But I can't. I spend a lot of time thinking about what the girls said and trying to figure out what I want to do about it all. Cole Devereaux's card has been folded and unfolded a hundred times.

On our second and final night in the city, Paige and I pick up sushi and bring it back to the hotel with a bottle of wine. We lounge in our robes, eating and drinking. Paige is far more relaxed and open than I've ever seen her, but still intelligent and insightful as ever.

"You know, many people believe home is not a place, but rather a person."

It's the first time she's brought up Ethan, and I almost choke on my smoked salmon roll at how direct she is.

"Umm, yeah. I know, I kind of believe that." I quickly drink some water and put my food to the side.

She looks at me over her plate of food. "Is it not plausible that just as Ethan is a physical manifestation of home for you, you are one for him?"

I nod, slowly, still uncertain where she's going. This isn't anything I haven't thought about myself.

"Therefore, is it not equally plausible that when faced with the risk of losing his home, the most important person in his life second to none except maybe his sister, he panicked and acted irrationally?

"You guys said all this before we left Dogwood Cove."

Paige nods thoughtfully. "We did. And it bears repeating."

That's the end of the conversation. Paige moves on to filling me in about the authors she hopes to meet tomorrow, and the books she's looking to get in stock at her store. I pay attention with only half of my mind, the other half going over what she said, what all of my friends have said.

Maybe I do need to give Ethan another chance; I need to give *love* another chance. He is my home, after all.

Later the next day, Paige and I arrive home with a car full of books for her store and a little bit of clarity for me. She parks in front of the bookstore, and I help her unload some of the many boxes of books piled high in her car.

"Thanks for taking me with you," I say when we finish. "I needed that distance from everything."

Paige looks at me thoughtfully. "I'm glad you came, and I hope you found some of the clarity you needed."

I nod and give her a grateful smile.

"Do you know what you're going to do?"

"About Ethan, or about Devereaux?"

Paige looks at me, surprise evident on her face. "I didn't realize Devereaux was an option."

I shrug, unsure how to verbalize the one question that still remains. "It wasn't. But..." my voice trails off as I glance down.

"But now you wonder if selling, and leaving, might be the best choice if Ethan can't love you the way you want to be loved?"

I shift on my feet, uncomfortable that she figured it out so easily. "I mean, yeah, sort of. The thought did cross my mind once or twice. I don't want to leave," I say quickly, beginning to pace back and forth in front of Paige. "But how hard is it going to be if I stay here and have to see him all the time? If we're both in the same town, but not together?"

"Are you saying you haven't forgiven him?" She sounds confused.

"That's not what I meant. I have forgiven him, I just..." My voice trails off, because I don't know what to say. "I forgive him for lying. I understand why he did it. But can I move on from him not trusting our relationship enough to know that I would stay? That's the part I'm not so sure of. Because what if he never trusts us? I can't live in a relationship where one person is always scared it's going to end somehow."

Paige nods, and her expression turns thoughtful. "I understand. I hope you know that we would all be very sad if you left. And if I may say one final thing, do you think you can find it in yourself to give Ethan another chance to prove himself?"

I feel my eyebrows furrow. "What's going on, Paige?"

"I can't say anything," she says, shaking her head. "Just go next door and find Mila before you do anything else, okay?"

Confused, I nod. "Yeah. Fine. I'll go there now if you're good?"

Paige nods. "Yes, thanks for your help unloading. Bye!" She pivots on her foot and walks to the back of the store, leaving me alone.

That was definitely weird. But with Paige you never know what's coming. I leave the bookstore, still carrying my bag from the trip to Vancouver, and go next door to The Nutty Muffin. It's pretty empty inside, but I can see Mila. I push open the door, the chime tinkles, and she looks up. When she sees that it's me, her eyes widen, and she smiles.

"Summer, you're back. Did you guys have fun? Have you been to the resort? Of course not, you still have your bag." She laughs, but just like Paige's nervous tone earlier, Mila's laugh sounds anxious.

"Yes, I'm back, yes, we had fun, no I haven't been to the resort. What the heck is going on?"

Mila walks behind the long counter and pulls out a white envelope. "My job is to give you this."

"Your job..." I say slowly, confusion building in my mind.

"Yup. Want a muffin? I saved some from this morning."

"Sure," I reply, taking a seat in my favourite blue chair by the window. A couple of minutes later, Mila drops off a muffin and a coffee, and sits down across from me.

"I know I said this before you left, but I'm going to say it again. My brother was a total idiot. You have every right to be mad at him." She pauses, taking a big breath in and out. "And I really hope you give him another chance."

As I watch, Mila's eyes get glassy with unshed tears. "Don't get me wrong, Serena and Paige are great. But you? You're like my sister. We grew up together. When you left, I was devastated. And if Ethan's stupidity chases you away again, I will be heartbroken. I don't want to lose you. So, no matter what you decide about being in a relationship with him, please don't leave again, okay?"

I let out a low chuckle. "What is with you Monroes, thinking I'm going to leave?"

I reach over for her hand, taking it and holding it in my lap. Mila looks up at me, hope shining through her tears.

"I've almost forgiven your brother, give me a minute on that, okay? But I never planned on leaving. I had a moment while I was in Vancouver when I wondered if it would be too hard living here and not being with Ethan, but as soon as we got home, I knew I could never leave Dogwood Cove again. Talking about it with Paige helped, too. I've got friends here, a life here," I squeeze her hand, feeling more damn tears form. "I've got family here. I'm not leaving."

Mila launches herself out of her chair and into me, making me laugh.

"Okay, okay, get off of me, silly."

She leaps off of me and pulls me to stand. "Read the letter, Summer." With one final hug she turns and leaves me alone with my muffin, my coffee, and this mystery letter.

When I unfold the paper inside, for a brief moment my mind flashes to the last time I received an important letter. The one from George Hendrix, telling me about my dad. At the time, that letter devastated me. But now I can see how it brought me home.

Dear Summer,

I wish I knew how to start this letter, shorty, but I don't. You see, I've figured out that words are not enough. You told me you don't trust my words anymore, and I don't blame you. I screwed up, and words – or in my case, not using them, were to blame. So, here's the thing. I'm not going to use words to beg for your forgiveness one more time, to tell you how much I love you, or how much I want you in my life forever. I'm going to use actions.

If you're willing to give me another chance, please come and find me at Oceanside. Let me show you how I love you.

Always and forever,

Ethan.

Well, crap. Now I'm crying, *again*.

"Are those happy tears or mad tears?" Mila asks from behind the counter.

I look up at her and smile. "Happy."

"Then get over to the resort."

Dusk is falling by the time I get to Oceanside, because despite every part of me wanting to rush straight over, I decided to take the time to drop my bag off at my apartment and have a shower. I needed to make sure I was going to see Ethan with a clear head.

Turns out waiting was a good idea. Because the sight in front of me would not have been nearly as beautiful without the fading light of early evening.

I park beside Ethan's truck and follow a path of candles in small glass jars, the flames flickering. They lead me to the first cabin, the one that holds so many memories. Ethan being scared by the raccoons, our sleepover under the stars, and now this. The man I love standing in front of it, watching me, with a smile so full of love on his face, I might burst.

Chapter 24

Ethan

"I was starting to worry you weren't coming," I say, holding my hands nervously in front of me. God, I want to touch her. I want to pull her into my arms and reassure myself that she's really here.

Summer smiles at me, a soft, loving smile that puts me at ease instantly. "Sorry. I needed a few minutes to..." She shrugs. "I just needed a few more minutes."

"That's okay, as long as you're here now," I say hoarsely, silently willing her to take the last few steps that separate us. She bites her lip, and gazes around at the candles that I spent forever setting up. As soon as Mila texted me that Summer had left the bakery, I got to work. Hopefully, once she sees everything I've done, it'll be worth it.

"This is beautiful, Ethan. And your letter. Your letter was perfect."

"I told you, I know I need to use more than words to show you how much I love you. But you still deserve the words. I'm so sorry, Summer. I should have trusted in us, in what we were building. Instead I let fear get in the way. I didn't even know I was scared to love someone, much less scared to lose them, until you. I promise I'll do whatever it takes to prove to you that I'm in this one hundred percent. No more secrets."

When I say that, she looks up and walks over, her hand fluttering out to rest on my chest. She's so close I can smell her minty floral aroma, that delicate, fresh, beautiful scent that is Summer.

"You don't have to prove anything to me. I don't like what you did, but I can understand why you did it. But the thing is, Ethan, love is a risk. There's always a chance you'll lose someone you love." She steps back, her arms folding in front of her chest, and I hate how much I ache from not feeling her touch. "You should have told me about Aubrey. It makes sense that you were worried about me leaving after what she did so soon after your parents died."

I stare at her in wonder. How does she see it so clearly when I didn't?

Then Summer closes the short distance between us, and reaches her arms up and around my neck. "But I'm not planning on going anywhere, Ethan." Lifting up onto her toes, she kisses me at last. It's sweet and tentative at first, as if we're relearning each other, building back the bond of love we were creating before everything went wrong. I hold back, letting her take the lead. But when she opens her mouth, and her tongue softly strokes my lips, I welcome her in with a groan. My hands find their way to her hips, pulling her flush against my body. It's been less than a week, yet I've been empty without her. Now, I can sense my heart and soul repairing themselves, and filling with the taste and feel of her in my arms again.

In the back of my mind, I know I have so much more to show her, so I reluctantly pull away.

"Come with me, shorty," I whisper against her lips. Then, taking her hand, I turn and go up the steps to the front door of the cabin. "I had some help with this, just so you know. There's a lot of people that want to see you succeed."

Her brow is furrowed in confusion, but it quickly softens into surprise and happiness when I push the door open, turn on a switch, and she takes it all in.

The cabin is bathed in light, illuminating everything I've worked on these last few days. I tried my best to follow the design ideas Summer had shared with me, keeping everything light and airy, with an ocean theme in mind. The furniture is comfortable and eclectic, the bedspread a pale blue to match the cushions on the couch. Shelves on the wall are a mixture of nautical and aquatic décor, like shells and anchors, with some books about the area stacked up on one shelf for visitors to enjoy.

Summer turns in a slow circle, and her smile grows and grows.

"Ethan, it's perfect." She walks around the one-room cabin, trailing her hand over everything. Pausing at a lamp with rope wrapped around the base, she turns to me. "There's electricity. How is there electricity?"

"Reid and I got it all hooked back up."

"No, I mean, how did you pay for it?" She's starting to look concerned, so I pull out the final piece of my plan.

"Mrs. Henderson wanted me to give you this. Just know it's not a joke, and she'll explain everything."

I give her the cheque, and watch her eyes widen in disbelief when she sees the amount written down.

"What? This...this is a lot of money. How can she give this to me? Why?"

I put my hands on her shoulders and guide her to sit down on the couch. "She'll explain it all, but let's just say she was going to be your dad's silent partner. When he died, she decided to pass on her support to you."

"But this will pay for everything." When she looks back at me, she's glowing. "Ethan, with this I can open the resort, and soon!"

"I know, babe," I say with a smile. "That's what I wanted to show you with this cabin. You can make your dad's plan come to life. And I want to be right here beside you every step of the way."

Summer drops the cheque and throws herself at me. I catch her and settle her in my lap as she hugs me tightly. I can feel her heart beating strong and steady, and I finally let myself drop the last weight of worry and guilt.

"Thank you," she mumbles into my shoulder, before lifting her head to look at me. "I love you, Ethan Monroe.

It's the first time she's said the words, and it's every bit as perfect as I thought it would be.

"I love you, too. And I always will."

"Always and forever, right?" she says with a smile, repeating back the words from my note to her.

"Always and forever."

This time when we kiss, I take control, drinking her in deeply. Then I stand up, taking her with me, and walk over to the bed where I slowly lower her down before finally taking my lips off of her.

"Want to christen the bed with me?" I waggle my eyebrows and earn the sweet giggle I was hoping for. Instead of answering me with words, Summer lifts the bottom of my shirt up and off my body before running her hands up my torso to reach my shoulders.

The look she gives me is all the signal I need. Our clothes come off in a frenzy and soon she's stretched out underneath me, her body glowing in the soft light.

"Summer," I murmur softly as my hand strokes the hair back from her face. She pulls me down for a long, slow kiss that only breaks when my dick finds its way between her legs and I feel the wet heat waiting for me there. I move down her body slowly, dropping kisses everywhere I can as she writhes underneath me like the wanton goddess she is. When I reach the center of her arousal, I run my nose along the crease of her inner thigh, breathing in the scent of Summer and sex.

"Oh God, Ethan, please," she starts to plead, her fingers winding through my hair. I lift my head up to see her gaze burning into me.

"I've got you, babe."

"Yes," she breathes, falling back on the pillow. I lower my head and flatten my tongue against her, licking up her engorged slit slowly. That one taste is enough to make my cock throb, but I'm not moving until she's come at least once. With my thumb I massage her clit as my tongue darts in and out of her in shallow strokes. She makes a whining noise and her thighs clench and release. Every part of her is worshipped by my tongue in long lazy swirls and light sucks. When I slide two fingers inside, her body welcomes me easily. I can feel her muscles tighten almost instantly, but that's not good enough for me, so I blow a puff of air onto her clit, making her cry out.

"I can't, oh God, Ethan, I need to come, please...now...please..."

"Yeah, babe, let me hear you," I groan before doubling down my efforts until she starts to keen out my name. Seconds later her hands clutch my hair, and her legs start to squeeze my shoulders as she shudders and convulses from her orgasm.

I make my way back up Summer's body until I'm stretched out on top of her, holding most of my weight off her by propping up on my elbow. Her eyes open and she gives me a hazy, satisfied smile.

"Yes ma'am, you are welcome," I say with a chuckle. She weakly slaps at my chest with a giggle before pushing harder so that I roll over, taking her with me. Once she's straddling my legs, she licks her lips with a wicked grin. Bending down, her hair falls like a golden curtain around us as we kiss. She reaches a hand between our bodies and takes hold of my cock, stroking it from root to tip several times, making me groan into our kiss.

"I need you Ethan." Her words come out as a moan.

"Fuck, babe," I groan as she takes my dick and brings it to her entrance, lowering her body onto me slowly.

She lets out a soft sigh once she's fully seated on me, dropping her head down to her chest and slowly rocking her hips back and forth. Being with her like this, bare, nothing between us but our love, it's everything. Every emotion in the universe, all wrapped up into one perfect moment.

My hands go to her ass, then up over her hips until I cup her breasts, squeezing them, pinching her nipples and bringing a gasp to her lips. Contracting my stomach, I rise up to capture a breast in my mouth, kissing and sucking one while still caressing the other with my hand. Summer holds onto my shoulders and continues to move up and down my shaft. Our position, entwined on the bed like this, is intimate and close. I can't tell where she ends and I begin, and that's how I want us to be forever. Always connected, never ending.

"Fuck, babe." Those two words are all I manage to growl as Summer changes the pace on me. Slow and sweet turns into hot and frantic. She starts to bounce up and down on me, her inner walls squeezing my dick tight. My mouth returns to her breasts, biting, sucking, licking, loving every damn inch of her.

"Ethan, now, take me now."

I will do anything she asks of me. Anything. Especially this. Holding onto her, I flip us back over so that she's on her back. Her legs instantly wrap around my waist, her ankles locking behind me, her heels digging into my ass. I start to pump my hips in and out, slowly picking up speed until my thrusts are making the bed rock underneath us.

"Yes! Oh, shit yes, Summer. Fucking hell." I can't control the words falling out of my mouth anymore. My climax is hurtling toward me, and I can feel the telltale tightening of Summer's hips that let me know she's right there with me.

I push in once, twice, three more times before she screams, arching her back, and digging her nails into my back. I let out a guttural moan as I spill into her, letting this physical release also be the emotional one of everything that's held me back.

Summer Harris has healed me, when I didn't even know I was broken.

Right when I thought I had found heaven again waking up with Summer in my arms, she shows me how she can make mornings even better.

"Summer? What are you doing?" I say groggily as she licks my shaft, following her tongue with her hand, squeezing gently.

"Isn't it obvious?" she says with a wicked grin before lowering her mouth over top of my dick and taking me in deep.

"Holy hell, woman."

I'm awake now. Really awake. This is no dream; this is my reality and it's fucking amazing. There's no way I should be ready to come as quickly as I am, especially not after going three rounds last night. But I clearly underestimate the magic of Summer's mouth, because minutes later my body starts to tighten in anticipation.

"Summer, babe, stop." I try to pull her off, but she shakes her head and hums around me. That vibration breaks me and my body jerks as I shatter. But she laps me up before crawling her way up my body, stretching out on top of me, resting her chin on her hands. I lift my head and kiss her, not even caring that I can taste myself on her lips.

"Can we do this every day?" I ask, tucking a piece of hair behind her ear.

She snorts with laughter, and I realize what I just said. "Not the blow job, babe, but waking up together."

Her smirk settles into a soft smile. "Yeah. I'd like that."

"Does that mean we can move your stuff into my house? Because the bed in that apartment is way too fucking small."

Epilogue

Summer

Today is my first Summer Solstice Festival since moving back to Dogwood Cove. I have vague memories of them as a child, but now as an adult I have a different appreciation. Seeing the kids running around with balloons and cotton candy, walking past the small petting farm, the vendors selling homemade wares and goodies. And my favourite part? The gorgeous man walking toward me with a sexy smile that's all for me.

"Hey, lumberjack."

Ethan dips me over his arm and kisses me right there in front of the gazebo. Everyone can see us, and I can't bring myself to care one bit. When he brings me back upright, he's grinning like a kid who just got a piece of his favourite candy.

"Two more hours and then we can go home, to *our* house," he says in the low voice that never fails to drive me crazy with lust.

"Are you ever going to stop being so excited about saying 'our house'?" I'm only half teasing. I truthfully love how excited he is that we are living together now. Any doubts I might have had about moving so quickly were dashed as soon as I walked in the door with my meager belongings. Ethan had moved a lot of his stuff out, and the next day we went shopping for things to *make it our place, not just mine* as he put it.

"Never." He punctuates the word with another kiss to my lips before looping his arm around my shoulders as we start to walk. The air is full of laughter and chatter, the smell of popcorn mingling with the sweet aroma of BeaverTails, those amazing and gigantic pieces of fried dough, so delicious and so reminiscent of every fair I've ever attended. My stomach rumbles at the thought of eating one.

"Cinnamon sugar or chocolate hazelnut?" I ask, earning a confused stare from Ethan. I giggle and slide my hand into his back pocket, pulling myself in even closer. "I'm buying us a BeaverTail."

"Oh, well in that case, OG babe. Cinnamon sugar."

We turn in the direction of the stall selling the treats and wait in line. People greet us, and even though I'm sure most of it is because I'm here with Mayor Monroe, it's nice to be included and welcomed. Every day something happens that reinforces to me that I'm in the right place, and I made the right decision. I look up at Ethan as he chats easily with someone who's come up to him with a question. My heart is so full of love for him.

The last few weeks went by in a flurry of activity. When I went over to Mrs. Henderson's house and heard the story of how she and my dad were going to be partners in the resort, it felt like one more sign that this was meant to be. Sure, a part of me wishes Dad had mentioned that situation in his will or something, but after talking to her about how important her privacy was to her, I get it. Still, it would have saved a lot of worry if I had known sooner. But now things are moving quickly. The cabins are all fixed up, and we're working on the main building. I've hired a marketing consultant to help come up with a plan to get us back out there and we've tentatively set August 1st as our reopening date. What no one other than Mrs. Henderson and the marketing consultant know is that I'm also planning a surprise barbecue to be held the week prior as a way to thank everyone who has helped me get to this point.

The fact that everything is happening in just over a month keeps me up at night sometimes, but Ethan has become very creative in ways to help me relax.

"Hi lovebirds!" Serena's voice carries over the crowd and I turn to see her walking over with Paige and Mila. Mila's got her dog, Milo, with her as usual. That dog goes everywhere with her, even to the bakery where he has a bed and is the unofficial greeter.

"Hey," I say in return, bending down to love on Milo. He really is a sweetheart. "How is his leg?"

Mila frowns. "He's still pretty stiff, but Jackson seems to think it'll get better over time."

Her face stays remarkably blank, even after mentioning the hot new vet in town. But I've noticed the two of them spending a lot of time together.

Before she can reply, it's our turn to order and I quickly step up to the vendor.

"One cinnamon sugar, please."

"Make it two," Serena pipes in. "Mila needs some sweetening up."

I hide my smile at that, but Ethan isn't so subtle as he chuckles out loud, earning a glare from his sister.

"Mila can make her own goddamn sugar-coated fried dough," the woman in question grumbles under her breath. But when Serena hands the still-steaming treat over to her, she doesn't hesitate to take a large bite.

We wander away as a group, and spend the next hour checking out the festival. A few people stop to ask how things are going at Oceanside and tell me how happy they are that I'm fulfilling my dad's plans. Every time this happens, my heart both breaks and fills. I'm so happy Dad had a good life after I left. This town took care of him, loved him, and supported him, even when he got sick.

Later on, Ethan pulls me over to the small stage that's set up. My jaw drops in surprise when Nash Parker, country music's newest superstar, and one of my favourite musicians of all time, walks onstage.

"Did you know he was playing?"

Ethan shrugs nonchalantly. "Well, let's just say I might know his drummer from college."

"Oh my God, Ethan!" I shriek right along with Mila, Serena, and half the audience as my favourite musician croons to everyone from up onstage. I can't believe this is really happening, and it only gets better when Ethan pulls me over to the group of musicians and introduces me to the man himself. It's all I can do not to trip over my words and make a complete fool of myself, that's how starstruck I am.

Eventually, everyone goes their separate ways. The fireworks are happening later tonight, but we're going home for awhile before that. When we pull up to Ethan's — I mean our — house, Ethan hops down from the truck and jogs around to my side. He opens my door, but instead of just letting me climb down, his hands go to my hips and he lifts me out of the truck and into his arms.

"We've got a couple of hours to ourselves and you taste so fucking sweet from that BeaverTail. Any objections to me taking you to bed right now?

I giggle. "None at all."

We missed the fireworks that night. Well, we missed the fireworks in town. We had plenty of our own, in the privacy of our bedroom.

"Remember when I said always and forever, shorty?" Ethan whispers into the top of my head as we lay tangled together in bed.

"You say it all the time, how could I ever forget?" I lift my head to smile at him. He quickly moves in and kisses my lips with a happy sigh. My eyes flutter closed as I revel in this moment. But when something cold slides onto my finger, they fly open.

"Ethan..." I look down at my hand where a beautiful diamond is blinking back at me.

"I know it might seem fast. But let's face it, I've known you my entire life. And I plan on loving you for the rest of it. This ring is my way of proving that to you, and I hope you'll accept it."

"Always and forever?" I whisper, feeling a smile stretch across my face.

Ethan nods. "Yeah, always and forever."

Thank you so much for reading *Always and Forever*. If you enjoyed it, please leave a review wherever you buy books.

Click HERE to pre-order *Rumours and Romance*, the second book in the Dogwood Cove series now for a special price!

If you want more Summer and Ethan, get your special bonus scene by signing up for my newsletter HERE or by visiting my website, at www.authorjuliajarrett.com

Acknowledgements

Thank you as always to my amazing husband and children who put up with Mama working all the time and stressing about deadlines! To my KKSB sisters, Mae, Chelle, Claire and Georgia - thank you for being my safe port in any storm, for dealing with my crazy, and supporting me always. To my incredible beta readers, Erica and Erin, thank you for pointing out my strengths and weaknesses in the best possible way. My editor, Chris, you made this story shine!

And of course, thank you to my team of advance readers. I don't know how I got so lucky to find all of you but I will be forever grateful for your support!

Also By Julia Jarrett

Dogwood Cove
Always and Forever
Rumours and Romance
Secrets and Mistletoe - A 12 Days of Kissmas Novella
Work and Play
Truth and Temptation
Love and Leashes – A Love At First Bark Novella, coming June 2022
Then and Now – coming fall, 2022

Westmount Island Novella Trilogy
Falling Fast
Falling Again
Falling Forever

Lucky Strike Lovers Quartet
Loving Callie
Protecting Anna
Serenading Reagan
Romancing Melanie

Standalone

Seductive Swimmer - A standalone novel set in the Cocky Hero World, inspired by Vi Keeland and Penelope Ward's Cocky Bastard series

About The Author

Julia Jarrett is a busy mother of two boys, a happy wife to her real-life book boyfriend and the owner of two rescue dogs, one from Guatemala and another one from Taiwan. She lives on the West Coast of Canada and when she isn't writing contemporary romance novels full of relatable heroines and swoon-worthy heroes, she loves to run, practice yoga, drink wine and read.

Follow Julia:

Instagram

Facebook: Julia Jarrett Reader Group

BookBub

GoodReads

Manufactured by Amazon.ca
Bolton, ON

26133538R00155